RAVE REVIEWS FOR T. M. WRIGHT

"T. M. Wright is a rare and blazing talent."

—Stephen King

"T. M. Wright has a unique imagination."

—Dean Koontz

"Like Stephen King at his best, Wright can hold us shivering on the edge between laughter and fear."

—*Newsday*

"T. M. Wright is a master of the subtle fright that catches you by surprise and never quite lets you go."

—Whitley Strieber

"Wright convincingly proves that he understands, as few do, how to give a scare wthout spilling blood all over the page."

—*Publishers Weekly*

"T. M. Wright is more than a master of quiet horror—he is a one-man definition of the term."

—Ramsey Campbell

"T. M. Wright's nose for horror is as acute as Stephen King's."

—*Fear*

"I have been an unabashed fan of T. M. Wright's since reading his first novel."

arles L. Grant

DEC 0

MORE PRAISE FOR T. M. WRIGHT!

"Without doubt, Wright is one of the most interestesting horror writers out there."

—*At World's End*

"A producer of work of the highest caliber. While many other authors may be sweating over their next supernatural extravaganza, Wright seems to deliver these delicious pockets almost effortlessly. His narrative is so sharp it makes a lot of writers seem clumsy by comparison."

—Horrorworld.com

"T. M. Wright is a brilliant writer. His impeccable prose is hypnotic and the rhythm of his words entrancing."

—*2 A.M. Magazine*

"Keep an eye on T. M. Wright."

—*The Philadelphia Inquirer*

"Wright's slow escalation of terror is masterly."

—*The Sun Times* (U.K.)

SHAPES IN THE DARKNESS

As Larry watched the people, as he was about to get out of the car and approach them to ask who they were and what in the hell they thought they were doing, they moved away from the light—two to the north, two to the south, and the thin, scruffy boy in Larry's direction, toward the light, as if he were drawn to it. And watching him, Larry could see, at last, what it was that was so frightening and so confusing about these people, and about this boy. They were approximations. Half-formed. Half-finished. Like oil paintings in progress. They had no eyes, only the suggestion of eyes, and no arms, or hands or legs, only the suggestion of arms and hands and legs. As if something real and tangible were moving behind a fogged window.

Larry lowered his head, covered his eyes with his fists, and screamed. . . .

THE HOUSE ON ORCHID STREET

T. M. WRIGHT

LEISURE BOOKS NEW YORK CITY

For Elizabeth Eastman

A LEISURE BOOK ®

November 2003

Published by

Dorchester Publishing Co., Inc.
200 Madison Avenue
New York, NY 10016

ISBN 0-8439-5090-0

Visit us on the web at www.dorchesterpub.com.

THE HOUSE ON ORCHID STREET

Part One
A House
With Stories to Tell

Chapter One
Gloria

1931

The woman was very fat. She sat naked in the
August heat, staining the green upholstered
Queen Anne chair with her sweat and smiling
broadly at the short, thin man across the big
room. The woman had her legs crossed, her huge
arms on the arms of the chair, and her head
tilted, as if she were affecting a fetching pose.
She had what would have been a pleasantly
pretty face were it not for her multiple chins and
eyes puffed nearly shut by obesity. Her name was
Gloria. The man across the room was painting
her portrait. His name was Llewellyn Simms, and
he was a very capable artist. He referred to his
style as "gross modernist." Its intention, he said,

was honesty: "If you see a wart, you paint it," he told students at his twice-weekly painting class. "And if you see disease, you paint it. Flattery is not art. Art is *life,* and all its pain and ugliness."

Gloria very much liked posing naked for Llewellyn. She liked the fact that he had to study her body closely in order to paint her, and that, when necessary, he chose to manually maneuver her into the positions he found most to his liking ("Lay hands on the thing you want to paint and you will know it better," he proclaimed).

Gloria was an articulate and intelligent woman. She lived alone in her mammoth house on Orchid Street. She had always lived alone in it, except for her first six months there, when she had seen to the care and feeding of her ailing father, a time that, she thanked her lucky stars, was far behind her.

Llewellyn Simms said to her, "Are you getting tired, Gloria? Do you want some tea?" In the summer, Gloria drank gallons of sugary iced tea.

"No," she answered. "Perhaps later." She waved luxuriously at his canvas. "How is it coming, Llewellyn?" Her voice would have been a high tenor were it not for rolls of fat that choked her larynx and deformed the shape of her mouth. What would have been a high tenor was a low, sputtering alto that was essentially sexless.

"How's it coming?" Llewellyn said. He frowned. On his face, the frown looked like a skeletal, slack-jawed pout. "It's not very good," he confessed. "It's too . . . *white!*"

Gloria chuckled, a noise that barely made it up out of her stomach, through her massive chest, into her throat, and out her mouth. It sounded like a gurgling whisper. "Llewellyn," she said, "*I'm* white!"

He smiled thinly, as if she had told him a joke and he didn't get it. "You are aware of course," he said, "that there are areas on your body, small, roughly circular areas that are closer to yellow than to flesh color, and of course you are aware that your skin is not all 'white,' per se—"

"Llewellyn, of course I'm aware of it."

"But I have done you all in white, today, and that is something I can not explain." His pout became very exaggerated. He looked on the verge of tears. "I have disfigured you."

"I don't want you to cry, Llewellyn."

"Oh, Gloria, I don't want to, either." His eyes watered; he made no effort to dab the moisture away; his arms hung limply at his sides. "Can I turn you around, Gloria? I would like to do you from the back."

"You can do what you have always done, Llewellyn. You can do with me whatever you

5

wish to do." And so he crossed the room very quickly, his eyes still watering, his pout quivering, and he took hold of her around the waist with his right hand, and under her arm with his left; then with her help he coaxed her out of the chair to a standing position and turned her around slowly, so her back was to him.

He told her, in a gush, "Your flesh is lovely! I love the movements of it!" and went back to his canvas and furiously obliterated the frontal view he had done and began on the rear view with the proper colors. His pout had vanished and he smiled as he worked.

The house that Gloria lived in on Orchid Street was very large, made of brick, a late Victorian beast that—when Llewellyn was not there painting her, and he painted her only once a week—she moved about in almost constantly, from room to room (there were seventeen of them) as if in search of something. She moved with much grace, despite her size, and she had learned how to maneuver herself about on the old floors without making much noise at all. It was a very unnerving thing to see.

Chapter Two

The real estate agent was a tall and flabby man named Lucien Straub who wore an ill-fitting blue leisure suit. He was coming down with a summer cold, so he let out with a vibrato honk periodically, then poked at his nose with a red and black handkerchief, and said in a hoarse whisper, "Beggin' your pardon."

It hadn't taken him long to show Katherine the outside of the house because it was small (*A Country Charmer,* the ad began), and because he had clearly wanted to get her inside it.

"You're alone, Miss Nichols?" he asked, his voice tinged with incredulity. He sniffled again, then took the house key from the lockbox just to the side of the front door.

"No, Mr. Straub," Katherine answered. She stood several feet to his right on the small, sturdy front porch (being close to him was unpleasant;

7

in the still summer heat the sickly sweet odor of his perspiration hung around him like a cloud). "I'm not alone."

He shoved the key in the lock, grinned at her, looked back at the door, and turned the key. "I mean, of course"—he pushed the door open—"that you're going to live here alone. That's what I mean. Nobody's going to be living here with you." He sniffled once more, whispered, "Beggin' your pardon," grabbed his red and black handkerchief from the jacket pocket of his leisure suit, and poked at his nose with it. Katherine felt momentary pleasure at his discomfort. "A summer cold," he explained, and held his arm out toward the inside of the house. "Go right in, please."

Katherine looked past him at the small foyer. She saw a closet to her right, a floor-standing mirror to her left. An open door several feet beyond led into the kitchen, and several feet beyond that the foyer opened onto a small living room. She saw the suggestion of a dark, floral-print couch and sheer white drapes on a set of tall windows.

She turned to Straub. "This house is furnished?" she asked.

He shook his big, angular head. "No, no, Miss Nichols. Of course it's not furnished."

She looked back at the inside of the house. It

was empty. "The artist's eye," she said.

Straub said, "Oh, you're an artist?"

She opened her mouth to answer, but could see at once that his question had merely been a courtesy, and he said again, "Go right in, please."

She stepped past him, into the house.

In Honeoye—an hour later

She was being watched from several different angles as she stood in the phone booth and searched her purse for change. Across the street, in front of the town's only pharmacy, a part-time laborer named Sammy was watching her with a flat smile of appreciation on his lips, because Katherine was a redhead. As he watched her, he thought, in so many words, *Can I help you, miss? Can I give you a quarter? Do you need a quarter?* He mentally rehearsed the questions a number of times, trying for the right inflection and pitch. He would watch and mentally edit his approach until she left the phone booth and drove off.

Mrs. Claire Wise watched her, too, from a booth in Phil's Restaurant (Phil had died three decades earlier; Clark, his son, has assumed ownership and operation of the restaurant). As Mrs. Wise pushed forkfuls of hot roast beef sandwich into her mouth, she catalogued all that was so obviously wrong with Katherine: *She's much too well endowed, of course!* was at the top of her list, followed by, *And she drives a foreign car.* Then, in response to something Lucien Straub had told her, *And everyone knows what artists are about, don't they!*

At last, Katherine found a quarter at the bottom of her purse, caught Claire's eye, smiled a little, became self-conscious because she could see that the woman was watching her every move, then made a collect call.

"Larry? Hi."

"I don't believe it."

"Don't believe what?"

"My God, Katherine—I thought you'd gone the way of the carrier pigeon. Where in the hell are you?"

"I'm in Honeoye."

"Where in the hell is that?"

"Downstate. Fifty miles." A short pause, then, "Larry?"

"I'm here." He sounded confused. "What's going on?"

"Larry, I'm moving out."

"Moving out? You mean out of the apartment?"

10

"Yes." She took a deep breath, then continued, on the exhale, "I'm sorry."

"I don't understand. Wait a minute. Is something wrong? What's wrong?"

"Of course something's wrong."

"You mean there's something wrong with *us*? I thought we were pretty solid. You mean we aren't?"

Katherine shook her head sadly. "I don't know, Larry. I'm not sure."

"And so you're going to move out? Great, that's just great. And thanks for the advance warning, by the way. Don't you think the adult thing would have been to talk face-to-face before you simply ran away? It's typical Katherine shit!"

"I want you to come down here, Larry. I'm buying a house."

"Oh, for God's sake—"

"It's a very nice little house. . . ."

" 'A very nice little house,' she says." He was mumbling to himself. It was a habit that she usually found cute and vaguely eccentric. Now, it annoyed her. "Larry," she said, "we've got to talk."

"*Now* she says we've got to talk! Christ! Sure, go ahead. Talk."

"Down here, Larry."

"No. Now. Say what you've got to say."

11

"I just want to live . . ." She faltered, then continued, ". . . alone."

"Christ, Katherine—why?"

"Why," she asked, "does anyone want to live alone?"

"What is this, twenty questions? How the hell do I know? I thought we were getting along okay. I thought we were solid as a brick, so how the hell do I know? Who the hell's a mind reader? I'm just the live-in boyfriend who's apparently as dense as a goddamned stump!" He was slipping into frustrated and angry incoherence, she realized. He went on more slowly, "No, Katherine, I'm sorry. Please. I'm sorry. You want to live alone? Fine. Good. You probably need it. I mean, if you *think* you need it, then chances are you do need it." Katherine supposed that he smiled to himself, pleased at this new tactic. "What are you talking about? A month, two months? Hell, I could take that much time off. I could find an apartment for myself there in Honeoye—"

"You're making this very difficult, Larry. I told you, I'm going to *buy* this house."

"Yes, I know you told me that. I was trying to ignore it because it's so . . ." Silence.

" 'Stupid,' Larry?"

"Irresponsible, immature. Stupid? No, I wouldn't say that. Yes, I would. Stupid. It's as stupid a thing as you've ever done, Katherine."

"Perhaps you're right, Larry. But it's something . . . it will be something of my own. That's important."

"What do you need, Katherine? Time to think? Because I can understand that. We all have to be alone. We all have to be alone to think. Hell, I know that I do, so why not you, right? Are we that different? Of course not. We may not share the same genetics, but we don't live on separate planets, either."

"You're babbling," she told him. She wished she could reach out and end his frustration and anger. She wished she could say, *This is a joke, Larry. I'm coming home.*

He said, "Yes, I know I'm babbling. Forgive me." A short silence, then, "You said you wanted me to come down there?"

His sudden change of mood surprised her. She supposed that she should have grown used to his mood changes by now, but she hadn't. "Yes," she said, "I'd like you to have a look at the house."

"You probably know as much about houses as I do, Katherine."

"Probably. But I'd still like you to have a look at it."

"Okay," he said.

"Okay?"

"Yes, I'll come down. Just don't expect me to like it."

At the house, sunset

She didn't much care for the windows; they were too close to the floor and too narrow, so they wouldn't let in enough light. Light was important to her.

She looked at her feet. She'd taken off her blue tennis shoes and was sitting on the living room's hardwood floor, her back against the west wall and her gaze on the east-facing windows. She was wearing faded, nicely fitted jeans and a sleeveless white cotton blouse. ("Of course you can wait at the house, Miss Nichols. Just drop the key off here when you're done." . . . "Thank you, Mr. Straub." . . . "It's nothing. Perhaps you'd like me to show you the way out there, again. I can wait with you until your boyfriend shows up." . . . "No, I think I can find my own way.")

She looked toward the ceiling and heard what sounded like the distant, polysyllabic cooing of pigeons—from within the attic, she guessed. And she remembered looking into the attic, no more than a crawl space, with Straub, several hours earlier, when he had pointed out the

14

mounds of shredded fiberglass insulation and had told her, "This house is real good and tight. You'll see when the winter comes." She lowered her head and focused on the windows again. They were indeed too narrow; they made the house look like a fortress. She decided that she'd have them widened when she moved in.

She thought that she'd enjoy living here. Alone. The house had the kind of atmosphere that her work needed—it was softly melancholy, like the poetry she used to write as a teenager, but, oddly, with something bright and hopeful about it.

She smiled—a good smile on an appealing face—and became aware that the darkness was catching up with her. She extended her arm, found the light switch, flicked it. One of two low-wattage bulbs in a brass ceiling fixture did what it could to bring light into the small room.

For a moment, the headlights of what she supposed was Larry's car played on the windows. She sighed, stood: "Jesus," she whispered, because she didn't look forward to the confrontation approaching. She made her way slowly to the front door, pulled it open.

She saw that except for her car, the narrow dirt road in front of the house was empty.

Chapter Three

. . . secluded but accessible, the ad for the house (which began, *A Country Charmer*) went on. And it was true. Even Larry Cage, whose sense of direction had never been much good, was finding the directions Katherine had given him pretty easy to follow: *South out of the city, on Route 46A, to Honeoye, about forty miles. In Honeoye, east to the end of Route 24 . . .*

He stopped the car, dug a flashlight out of the glove compartment, shone it on a battered street sign: GARNSEY ROAD, the sign read. "Good," he whispered, and turned onto the road. At once, he saw what he assumed were the lights of a house just beyond what appeared, in the darkness, to be a line of tall poplars some distance off. But the lights winked out and he found that Garnsey Road was too rutted to sustain even the posted speed limit of thirty. He slowed the car.

Moments later, he saw the vague dark outline of the house, then Katherine's ancient Corolla ("Jesus, Katherine," he had said to her a couple of weeks earlier, "why don't you get a halfway decent car?" . . . "Because," she'd answered, "I'm comfortable with *that* car, Larry." But, after a little pushing from him, she'd promised to "look for something else").

He pulled up behind the Toyota, honked his horn once, and got out.

He knew what he was going to say to her. He'd been honing it to a keen, incisive precision: "Let's get married. Right now, Katherine. Tonight, if possible." That would probably do the trick, he decided, because she had always been quite pliable, and she admired directness, so such directness, from him, would be charming and unexpected and would take her by surprise.

He looked at the house. He wished that it were still daylight, so he could see it better, then decided that it didn't matter, because Katherine wouldn't be spending much time in it—at least not if *he* had any say in the matter.

A picket fence stood in front of the house (in the darkness, Larry couldn't be sure of its color—he supposed it was white). He fiddled with the latch on the fence gate. "Katherine?" he called. He opened the latch, pushed the gate open, and made his way down a weathered fieldstone walkway to the bottom of the front porch steps. He glanced about, taking in the feel of the house. He thought he understood why Katherine had decided so very impulsively to buy it—not simply because she was, by nature, impulsive, but because the house had an air of comfort and livability about it. It would be a great place to spend a cold winter night.

"Hi," he heard then. It was Katherine. He looked to his right, toward the source of her voice, said, "You scared me," and grinned a boyish grin. He could barely see her. She was seated at the far end of the porch and was looking toward the road.

"I didn't mean to scare you," she said, her gaze still on the road. She moved her arm a little, to indicate the house. "Do you like this place, Larry?"

He moved slowly, as if in thought, up the three porch steps. "It's got a nice feel to it, sure," he said, and stopped. He was facing the front door. He put his hands into his pockets, lifted his head slightly. "You've got to get rid of that old rust bucket, Katherine."

"I'm going to buy this house, Larry," she said.

He turned his head to look at her. He could see her more clearly, now. She was in a dark wicker chair and her feet were flat on the porch floor, her hands flat on the arms of the chair. Her gaze was still on the road. He wished she'd look at him. "We're not even going to talk about it?" he said.

She looked at him, then at the road again. "No," she answered with finality. "Not about that, anyway."

He sighed.

She added, "We aren't going to talk about it, Larry, because I'm . . . afraid of you." She looked at him again for a moment.

He took his hands from his pockets, turned around, and sat on the porch floor, with his knees up, arms around them, and his back against the front wall. "Afraid of me?" he whispered. He had a vague idea what she was talking about and wanted her to elaborate.

"Yes," she said. "You're very persuasive. You're much *too* persuasive."

He said nothing. He'd heard this speech from her before and he thought it was best to simply let her repeat it, to unburden herself of it.

She went on, "You'll talk me out of this whole thing, if I let you—"

"Maybe that's the point," he interrupted, and held his hand up at once, palm out: "No, I'm sorry, Katherine. Please, go on."

20

"It's *not* the point, Larry! 'If I let you' is not the point at all. Christ, some people let . . ." She hesitated. "Some people let other people lead them around everywhere. That doesn't mean they have any special feeling—" She stopped.

Larry coaxed, voice trembling, "Yes, Katherine? Go on."

"Nothing," she answered. "I was babbling, like you do. Let's go inside."

" 'No special feeling,' Katherine?"

"I want to show you my house, Larry."

"And *I* want to talk." He could hear the anger in his voice and it surprised him. "*I* want to talk!"

She said nothing.

He said, "This is a very dumb thing you're doing." He was trying to control his anger, but it was all but impossible, now, because it was being fueled by his pain. "It's right up there with all the other dumb things you've done—" He stopped.

"What other dumb things, Larry?"

"I don't know," he answered, frustrated in his anger. "I don't know," he repeated, though, as far he was concerned, there were dozens of dumb things he could bring up (leaving her teaching position at the college to do freelance artwork, for instance, and that "abortion thing" as he called it, and her ten-month involvement with a

21

well-known and very destructive religious sect: It had taken her quite a long time to get over that one). "You're just so . . . easily led," he told her.

"Goddammit, Larry, *that's* the point! Damn it to hell, *that's* the point. I know how easily led I am. My God, do you think I'm stupid? I'm not stupid—"

"I know that, hon."

"Don't call me 'hon.' I don't like it!"

He looked at her, dumbfounded. "You never told me that."

"I never told you a lot of things. I was afraid to."

He looked away. "What's this now? Time for the bold and unvarnished truth?" He shook his head. "If so, let's please postpone it."

She said nothing.

After a moment, he said, "Like what things, Katherine? What things are you afraid to tell me?"

"I thought we were going to postpone it."

He harrumphed. "We're talking about our relationship, here. We're talking about . . . about being comfortable with each other. . . ."

"I really would like to postpone it, Larry. It won't do either of us any good right now. I asked you down here because I wanted you to look at my house." She'd begun to plead with him; he liked it. "So why don't you do that, Larry? Why don't you come inside and look at my house?"

He said nothing. He was considering a response. He sensed that she was particularly vulnerable at that moment, that all she needed was a little push. . . .

So he said, very steadily, his eyes on her— though in the darkness, her face was little more than a pale blur—"Let's get married. Let's get married right now, Katherine. Tonight, if possible."

He heard a small gasp come from her; it pleased him. "If I took you by surprise, I meant to." He looked toward the road. After a minute, he coaxed, "Katherine?"

And she answered at once, her tone very tight and hurt, "Sometimes, Larry, you really are a world-class asshole! My God, why do you think I came down here? As an invitation for you to rescue me? You've got a hell of an ego!"

He raised an eyebrow and managed an "I'm sorry" in the tone of a small child caught in some foul act by a domineering parent.

And Katherine added, "Yes, I will marry you, Larry."

He sputtered an incoherency, pushed himself to his feet—a grin of disbelief flickering on his face—and made his way over to her. He bent

23

over to kiss her. "Thank you," he whispered. And she turned her face away from him. He hesitated, confused, then straightened. "I don't understand . . ."

"I've got to do this first, Larry."

"Got to do what? Buy this goddamned house?" His anger was rising. "Why? To fulfill some misguided dream of independence, or just because you *can* buy it?"

"Maybe both of those things," she answered calmly. "And because I like the house and because I'd like to live in it for a while."

"Damn you!" he whispered.

"I'm sorry if all this upsets you, Larry."

"Damn you!" he said aloud.

She lowered her head but said nothing.

"Damn you, goddamn you!" He was shouting, now. "Grow up, Katherine. For Christ's sake, grow up! You're just like your fucking brother!"

She pushed herself quickly to her feet; the wicker chair slid backward a few inches and hit the wall of the house with a dull thud. Her right arm swung around and her open hand fell hard on the side of Larry's head. She was a strong woman and the blow pushed him toward the porch railing. He grabbed it, steadied himself, brought his hand up to his ear, felt a trickle of blood there. He opened his mouth to speak, said

24

nothing, then turned, walked stiffly to the top of the porch steps, and looked at her. With effort, he fought down an impulse to rush back and do to her what she had just done to him. Instead, he told her, "I'm sorry you did that, Katherine. I think *you'll* be sorry, too!" Then he stalked to his car and drove off.

Chapter Four

. . . unique, continued the ad for the house on Garnsey Road (which began, *A Country Charmer, secluded but accessible*), *moved to its present location a half century ago . . .*

It was a sultry Friday afternoon. Katherine was moving in today. She had her brother, Jason, to help her. He was in his late twenties, several years her senior, and he confessed to her now, in his best big-brotherly way, as they sat on the front porch and waited for the first furniture delivery, that he had never liked Larry Cage much, and that, he concluded, "Maybe you'll have a little room to breathe, now."

Katherine smiled a small, shallow smile—*It's all right,* the smile said, *I don't mind if you meddle.* Because, she thought with a little twinge, her brother often tried to make her business his business. *He's just being protective,* she had told herself more than once. She followed the movements of a fat, pollen-laden honeybee in a dandelion patch nearby. She said, "I think I always knew you didn't care for him, Jason. I guess I chalked it up to jealousy."

Jason was quiet for a moment, then, after a chuckle, said, "Keep my cute little sister all to myself, you mean?" He paused a moment, then went on, "I never trusted him much. I think I saw some of my own shortcomings in him, magnified."

She patted his hand. "You don't have any shortcomings, Jason."

He chuckled again. "Would that it were true." He watched the honeybee, too. It was only a couple of feet away, buzzing frantically. "I saw a lot of selfishness in him, Katherine. A lot of possessiveness." The honeybee dipped, then recovered. "I mean, as far *you* were concerned, and *your* needs."

She looked at him, confused.

He went on, "Remember when you got hooked up with that religious group?"

A look of regret sped across her face. "How could I forget?" she said, and she remembered quickly the feeling of being dragged about, of being pushed around, being exhausted and helpless, and, on top of it all, a feeling that she

28

actually *liked* it, when she knew that deep within herself, she was screaming for release. "How could I forget?" she repeated.

Jason said, "Okay, did you ever stop to think why you got hooked up with them?" The honeybee landed on a dandelion. Its frantic buzzing stopped.

"Of course I did, Jason."

"And?"

"And I came to the conclusion that I needed something . . . to cling to." She focused on the honeybee clinging to the dandelion.

"And how did Larry figure into it?"

"I don't think he did. It was my problem, my solution." The honeybee took flight again, yellow pollen covering it like a sweater. It dipped from the excess weight, recovered, dipped again.

"You don't think he figured into it?" Jason said.

She tilted her head, as if in reflection. "Maybe a little. In the sense, I mean, that anybody I happened to be living with at the time—even you— could have figured into it."

"Uh-huh." He was clearly unconvinced. He watched the honeybee make a wide turn, buzzing frantically again, and head his way. "When is that damned truck supposed to show up?" he said.

Katherine looked at him, confused by his sudden anger. "Something wrong?" she asked.

"No. Just the heat," he mumbled. The honey-bee made tight, lumbering circles near his shoe. "Just the heat," he reiterated, and quickly lifted his foot and brought it down on the bee.

Katherine grimaced. She said, voice tight, "They told me three o'clock, Jason. Just a few more minutes."

"Rain," he said, at a whisper.

"Sorry?"

"We need some rain," he said aloud, as if sharing some great truth with her, and he nodded at the sky. It was spattered here and there with the wispy, dirty-cream-colored clouds common to hot and humid summer days. "We need some rain, sis," he repeated.

They both heard the distant grumble of a truck. Jason stood, took one step up to the porch, and looked south, toward Post Road. The noise of the truck grew steadily louder. Jason said, "I don't see him, yet."

Katherine said, "It might be someone out on that other road."

"You think so?"

The noise of the truck stopped. Jason looked toward the end of the porch. "Is there a road out there?" he asked.

"Out where?"

He nodded at the line of poplars. "Out there. Beyond those trees."

"No," Katherine answered. "I don't think so. I'm not sure."

"Because it sounded like that truck stopped there."

"Do you see it?" She joined him on the porch.

"No," he said.

"Me neither."

The first furniture delivery to the house on Garnsey Road was made a half hour later, much to Jason's indignation. "Part of what you're paying for, sis," he said later—in explanation of why he'd had angry words with the deliverymen—"is courtesy. And courtesy involves being on time. *Your* time, Katherine, and *my* time is worth just as much as—probably a lot more than—theirs."

By nightfall, most of the furniture had been uncrated, some of it had been put where Katherine wanted it, and Jason had left for home.

Chapter Five

Later that evening

. . . *a house with stories to tell,* the ad (which began, *A Country Charmer, secluded but accessible, unique—moved to its present location a half century ago*) went on to say.

Katherine's first find was a utility bill dated August 12, 1931, for $3.50 electric, and another bill that totaled $5.00 for coal. She found these bills in an upstairs closet on a high shelf where she also found the remains of a rag doll. Mildew had been working on it for quite some time and it was missing much of its cloth face, both its cloth arms, and its stomach. She realized with a little shudder that rodents had been chewing on it. She took it downstairs and tossed it into a grocery bag she was using as a trash container in the kitchen. She wrote, in big block letters on a blackboard she had hung in the kitchen, GET A TRASH CAN. She had never before used such methods to remind herself of things; it was one of the "simple changes" that she was making in her life. "Buying the house," she had told Jason, "was the first change, the most important change. And Larry"—she couldn't bring herself to use phrases like *splitting up with Larry*—"was the second." She had grinned ruefully. "It's very tiring not being who you really are. I need some rest."

She had gone on a tour of discovery in the house. The utility bills and the remains of the doll had been her first discoveries, and they had disappointed her. She'd wanted to find something less mundane—a bunch of letters tied with twine and sealed with red wax, perhaps.

Two of the other upstairs closets, one in the master bedroom and another, very shallow, like a linen closet minus shelves, had been empty. Way back in the largest of the upstairs closets, however, she had found a painting. It was small and had been put in a simple dark wood frame, then wrapped in burlap. It was a rendering, in oils, of an obese naked woman, hands clasped and feet together, seated in a delicate Queen Anne chair. The artist—whose name Katherine could see in the painting's lower left-hand corner, though it was illegible—had left little space for anything but the woman. Her massive arms crowded the sides of the canvas, her head—fringed by short black hair—hit the top of the canvas, and her toes disappeared under the bottom. Her skin possessed a slight bluish tint, though all of the other colors seemed natural enough—deep green eyes, dark red areolas and nipples, slightly lighter red lips. Katherine studied the painting for some time and decided that she liked its realism, and that she liked the woman, too, who seemed strangely comfortable and approachable. Beyond that, Katherine didn't much care for the angle the artist had chosen, as if he was looking at his subject from somewhere below and a couple of feet out from the woman's knees, or the fact that the woman's body crowded the canvas, which merely accented her almost grotesque obesity. It was a good artistic tactic, Katherine thought, but it wasn't very appealing. She covered the painting with the burlap in which she'd found it wrapped and stuck it back in the closet.

It was a small house and fifteen minutes after she'd started her tour of discovery it was complete. And that disappointed her, too, because now she'd have to finish straightening the furniture around, and that was a process that spoke of permanence and commitment. It said loudly that she was alone here. It said that Larry Cage had gone his way and she had gone hers. At last.

She went to the sink and turned the cold-water tap on, then the hot. She waited. The water from the hot tap stayed cold. She washed her hands with the cold water and went to the blackboard: CALL PLUMBER IN A.M., she wrote. She thought a moment and added, WHEN PHONE'S PUT IN. And then, beneath it, in very small, pinched letters, as if in afterthought, SOMETIME TOMORROW, MAYBE. WHO KNOWS WHEN?

The side door, to the left of the blackboard—which was hung at eye level—had a large window in it. The window was uncovered. Though she had bought curtains for it, she'd decided to exchange them for something a little less fussy. She could see a soft pattern of lights in the darkness beyond the window, now, and she focused on it a moment, interested in how the night looked here, behind her new house. Then she made her way reluctantly into the living room to finish straightening up. She muttered a playful curse at Jason for not sticking around.

Later that night

She knew she couldn't sleep, because the day had been big and important, the culmination of two weeks of bustling from here to there, from furniture stores to the real estate agent's office, to her lawyer's office, to Larry's apartment, again and again and again, tidying up all the gritty loose ends. It was those loose ends that were getting her down—all the memories and feelings and hurt from their two and a half years together. It all added up to the fact that she had been used. That she had allowed it. That she had *wanted* it. Now, in this house, she was going to get a chance to grow up. To be herself at last. It wouldn't be easy, she knew, because even at that moment, with all the tidied-up loose ends still gnawing at her, she wanted Larry in the bed with her. Beside her, at least, so she could reach over and touch him. She wanted to say to him, "So how do you like it?" And she wanted him to say, "Your house? I like it a lot." Because she did like it, and because his approval had always been important. "Damn it," she whispered, because she'd just brushed up against a truth that made her feel as if she was dealing with someone she didn't know at all well, and probably never would.

"So how do you like it?" she whispered, and listened to the silence in her house.

Dawn

She hated waking with the sun in her face. Through the window glass the heat and the light were magnified, and she turned violently away, cursing under her breath. She let her eyes open. What a hell of a way to begin her first full day in her first house, she thought, turned back, and let the sunlight wash over her. After a minute, she told herself that it felt good.

From below, and outside the house, she heard a soft tinkling noise, like glass rubbing against glass. She turned her face away from the sunlight and looked toward the north-facing window. She listened. The noise stopped. She threw the top sheet off—the night had been much too warm to sleep under a blanket—made her way to the window, and looked out. She saw the porch roof and the dandelion-choked front yard, the weathered fieldstone walkway, the picket fence, the narrow dirt road beyond, the fields and woods beyond that. And she smiled to herself, noting dimly the movement of her mouth in the reflection from the window, because she was standing naked at the window, which was a small fantasy she had always wanted to fulfill. Here, with the nearest house almost a mile away, she could fulfill it. Here, she could do pretty much what she wanted to do. She had twenty-eight acres in which to do it.

"Hi," she heard from behind her. She stiffened. Her hands went to the sides of the window and gripped them tightly, although she had realized at once who it was in the bedroom doorway. "Christ, Jason!" she whispered.

"What're you doing, sis—giving the townies a show?"

"No." She was trying hard to control her anger. She turned and walked quickly to a closet, opened it, withdrew a robe, and slipped it on.

"Because they're out there, sis. The townies, I mean."

"No one's out there, Jason."

"Sure they are. Two hunters. I think they're hunting raccoons. That's what these people do in their spare time, isn't it?"

"I wouldn't know." She stayed quiet a moment and let her anger cool. Then she went, "What are you doing here, Jason?"

He grinned. He was a very big, broad-shouldered man, with a full head of light blond hair and the beginnings of a handlebar moustache, and when he grinned he was the very soul of charm, and knew it.

"My axle broke," he said.

She was incredulous. "How in the hell did that happen?"

"On one of your damned potholes."

"A pothole broke your axle?"

"It was a pretty deep pothole." He was still grinning, embarrassed. Her anger was beginning to fade. "It was the mother of all potholes, actually, and I hit it at about seventy, I guess. Lucky I didn't kill myself." He nodded toward the east. "Out there, on the paved road. About five miles from here. So I came back. You were asleep—the lights were out, anyway—and I walked in. You really should lock your doors, Katherine."

"Sure, Jason. I move out here and I'm supposed to drag my urban paranoia with me."

"Locking your doors at night does not constitute urban paranoia, sis. I mean, people are just as crazy out here as they are in the city—there are just fewer of them." He grinned again, as though what he'd just said were profound.

Katherine nodded. "Uh-huh, I suppose that's true, but when I came here, to this house, I left a lot of things behind me. Locked doors was one of those things." A brief pause, then, "You want some breakfast?"

His grin broadened. "It's all ready. Oatmeal, eggs, and English muffins. Just like old times."

"Old times?"

"Sure. Don't tell me you don't remember Mom cooking us oatmeal, eggs, and English muffins."

She remembered. "Uh-huh," she said.

"You had oatmeal," he explained. "Eggs and English muffins I had to get in town. I borrowed your car. The clutch is sticking, you know. Why don't you think about getting a decent car?" He turned suddenly and gestured to her to follow. "Well, c'mon, breakfast is getting cold and there's nothing quite as bad as cold eggs and oatmeal." He gave her a quick once-over. "By the way, you're really keeping yourself in shape, aren't you?" And before she could answer, he disappeared down the hallway.

"What time is it?" she called.

"What time is it?" he called back. "Close to ten."

She was confused. "How can it be that late? I just watched the sun come up." But he was making his way down the stairs, now, and she guessed that he couldn't hear her.

41

Chapter Six

Lucien Straub arrived at 11:30; he had some papers for Katherine to sign. "Nothing to worry yourself about," he said, and she said, "Let me be the judge of that." Her remark pleased her because it was so forthright and adult. "Sure," Straub answered, obviously amused, and explained the papers in detail. At 11:45, he climbed back into his ten-year-old Chrysler, did a ragged K-turn on the gravel road, and chugged off.

"My God, what a jerk!" Jason said.

"Not simply a jerk," Katherine corrected, "an asshole, too," and after they shared a laugh, she thanked him for being there during the man's visit. "And he's a *lecherous* asshole, as well," she said.

"Uh-huh," Jason muttered, and there was a clear note of strain in his voice. "Aren't they all?"

"No," she answered. "Not all of them." She

43

paused a beat and went on, in a lighter tone, "He told me something I wasn't aware of."

"Oh?"

They were on the porch. Katherine sat on the top step. She was dressed in a white cotton blouse and cutoff jeans. Jason sat beside her, close enough that they were touching at the thighs and shoulders. "Yes, he said that this house was moved here from the city in 1931."

"On a truck, you mean?"

She nodded. "I knew it had been moved, but I didn't know how far."

"It must have cost a bundle."

"I suppose it did. But it explains one thing—it explains the *feel* of the house. It's got a city feel to it."

Jason grinned. "Is that your artistic sensibility talking?"

She shrugged. "I guess so. I'm sorry you don't believe in it."

He laughed shortly. "I believe in it, Katherine. I always have."

She changed the subject. "Want to help me in the garden?" She pushed herself to her feet.

He looked up at her. "What are you going to do in the garden?"

"Get it ready. I'd like to plant some things in it."

He smiled. "You mean things like vegetables and fruit and flowers?"

"I've always wanted a garden, Jason, and now that I've got the room—"

"Oh, you've got more than enough room." He stood. After a moment's silence, a look of deep concern came over him.

Katherine said, "Is something wrong?"

He shook his head a little, stepped over to her, put his big hands on her shoulders; it was a very paternal and affectionate gesture. "It's a nice house, Katherine," he said. "It really is. And I hope to God you're going to be happy in it."

She grinned nervously up at him. "I think I'll be happy here, Jason. I'm sure I will." She stood on tiptoes and kissed him lightly on the cheek. She felt his body stiffen and she stepped away. "So, are you going to help me or not?"

He held his hand up, palm out, and shook his head. "What I know about gardening you could stuff in an olive pit. No, sorry, but I should get into town and see if I can get the damned car fixed. Do you have a phone yet?"

She shook her head. "Not yet. Today, I think."

He muttered a curse, then started down the porch, stopped, looked back. "Isn't there a house around here somewhere? Up that way, maybe?" He nodded toward where the road followed a

45

shallow incline, curving south. It was a bright, warm morning, and it was getting warmer by the minute.

Katherine shrugged. "Damned if I know, Jason. I know there's a farm about a mile off, and if I were to have to guess"—she gestured to the north—"I'd say that it's over that way, beyond those trees." There was a small stand of deciduous trees a half mile behind the house, just off the property line. "I think I remember Straub mentioning it. Want to borrow my car? Or better yet, I could drive you into town . . ."

Jason climbed the porch steps again, came over to her, put his arm around her waist. "No. Thanks anyway, but I think I'm in the mood for a hike. It's a nice morning."

"But you had a five-mile hike just last night," Katherine said.

He shrugged. "Yeah, but I got a lot on my mind. Walking always helps me think."

"A lot on your mind? Like what?"

"Nothing you'd be interested in. Really." And with that, he took his arm from around her waist, went quickly to the east end of the porch, jumped off, then walked about fifty feet to a small square plot of earth, where the weeds were particularly high.

"Is this the garden?" he called.

46

"Yes," Katherine called back. "It's doing well, isn't it?"

"Very well indeed. My sister the green thumb."

Katherine went to the edge of the porch, so she could talk to Jason without yelling too loudly. "She used too much fertilizer, I think. The weeds love it."

"She?"

"The woman who lived here before me."

"Oh? When was that?"

"A couple of years ago. She died out there, in fact."

"While she was gardening?"

Katherine nodded. "A heart attack."

Jason stared silently at the garden for a moment, then nodded at the trees a half mile behind the house. "You think that farmhouse is over that way somewhere, huh?"

"I think so. I heard a tractor over there, once."

"Uh-huh. Well, I hope you're right." He grinned, turned around, and started toward the trees, lifting his legs high through belly-tall weeds and over mounds of moist earth. Without looking back, he waved and shouted, "I'll call you. From my place."

Katherine called, "Okay, and watch out for the townies."

"Who?" He didn't look back, he kept walking.

47

"The townies, remember?" she called, and watched until he was halfway to the woods. She thought as she turned and started for the house that Jason really was a very nice man and that she did love him, but that she was happy to be alone again.

She wondered then how a person got a garden ready for planting, and what, exactly, she was going to put in it.

Chapter Seven

Katherine found that there wasn't much she could do in the garden without the necessary tools—a rake, a hoe, a spade, et cetera—so she spent half an hour mentally planning how she was going to space her crops, what they were going to be, exactly (corn, of course, and squash, and cantaloupe, maybe), and how much time she wanted to give to them, because it was just a hobby, after all.

When she turned, at last, to go back to the house, she saw a small shed about twenty-five yards away, lost in a tangle of vines and underbrush. She smiled. It would be a good place to keep her gardening tools, once she got them, and she thought abstractedly that she had failed to see the shed earlier not only because it was shrouded in vines and underbrush but because it was also a dull greenish yellow, so it blended with its surroundings.

She went to the shed—it stood at the front of the line of poplars to the west of the house—and peered in through its one small window. The window was dirt-streaked and the glass was of poor quality, but she could dimly see a bench attached to the shed's rear wall, and, in a far corner, what could have been a man's hat dangling from a large nail.

She tried the door. It wouldn't budge. Decades of wind and weather, she guessed, had warped it shut. Perhaps Jason could get it open.

She started for the house, stopped, heard someone running toward her, looked toward the side of the house. A boy appeared there. He was about sixteen, she thought, and he was dressed in a white T-shirt with a blue *H* imprinted on it, red jogging shorts that were clearly too large, because he pulled them up every few seconds as he ran, and pastel-green, ankle-high sneakers. He stopped at once when he saw Katherine and a look of great embarrassment swept over him. He lowered his head a moment, he was a couple of yards from her. He said, "I didn't know anyone was living here again. I'm awful sorry."

"Sorry for what?" Katherine asked.

He looked as if the question had been impossibly stupid. "For . . . trespassing," he stammered.

"I don't mind," she said, stepped forward, and extended her hand. He stared at it a moment, then gripped it softly, as if he might hurt her. She gave him a warm smile. "My name's Katherine Nichols. I just moved in. Last night was my first night here, in fact."

Another quick look of embarrassment passed over him and he abruptly let go of her hand.

"Is something wrong?" Katherine asked.

He looked away, pulled his shorts up, looked back.

Katherine added, "Are you jogging?"

He shook his head briskly.

"You're running, then?" she added.

"Yeah," he said. "We don't call it jogging. That's for old people." He paused, then hurried on, "Beggin' your pardon," which was a phrase that the real estate agent used, so it made Katherine suddenly uncomfortable with this boy. She forced herself to smile again. "Are you on the track team or something?"

He shook his head. "We don't even have a basketball team. I run because I like it. Everyone likes to run."

Katherine nodded toward the stand of woods. "Is that where you run to?"

The boy hiked his shorts up again and pointed at the line of poplars. "Yeah, along there," he explained. "Alongside those trees, then down into the woods, up and around to Tom Haislip's farm." He pointed to his left. "And then home." He smiled proudly. "It works out to almost ten miles, and I run it three or four times a week. My dad says that maybe the people that put on the Olympics will catch wind of it. He says you never know. And I guess that's true."

Katherine nodded. "Yes," she said, "I suppose it is." A brief pause. "At any rate, please feel free to use my property"—the phrase sounded alien to her—"whenever you'd like."

He gave her a broad, thankful smile. She thought, *He's a very good looking boy,* and tried to chase the thought away at once; she wasn't sure why. He stuck his hand out; she took it. He squeezed it hard. "Thanks, Miss Nichols."

"Katherine," she said.

"Sure," he said, let go of her hand, then abruptly took it again. "I'm William Straub." She winced. "But you can call me Bill. I'm real pleased to meet you." He let go of her hand and began running in place. "It's real nice of you to let me keep running here, 'cause the only other path is way down that way"—he inclined his head to the right—"about a mile, and it's pretty rough, you know. I nearly busted my shinbone on it, once, not that Mrs. Gore much cared."

"Mrs. Gore?"

"The woman who lived here a couple years ago, the one who died. She said"—he quickened his pace—"that I shouldn't run out here, so I didn't. I used that other path, 'cause my dad—he's a real estate agent."

"Yes, I know."

"He says"—he quickened his pace again, so his words began hiccoughing out of him—"you got to . . . respect people's . . . property rights, and I guess it's . . . true, and besides she was pretty firm . . . about it, you know, awful . . . firm, so"—he turned so he was facing the line of poplars as he ran in place—"I used the . . . other path, like I . . . said, for a while, till she . . . died, and then I started . . . using this one . . . again, and I'm . . . glad, real . . . glad you're gonna let me . . . keep using it. Gotta go!" And he was off.

Katherine called after him, smiling, "It was nice meeting you," but received no reply.

At 2:30, Katherine's telephone was installed. At 4:00, she checked for a dial tone, as she'd been instructed, heard nothing, tried again at 4:30, still heard nothing ("Sometimes the switching at the main office gets a little more complicated than we like," the installer told her, "so sometimes the phones don't get turned on exactly when we say they will. You just got to be patient."), and again at 5:00 and 5:30 and 6:00. At 6:15, her anger mounting, she picked up the receiver and heard a dial tone. She called her brother's number, got no answer, hung up. Odd that he hadn't reached home yet. She called a plumber in Honeoye about the water heater, got an answering service, and left a message. Less than a minute later, the phone rang. It sent a little shiver of pleasure through—her first phone call in her first house. It was an event.

She answered the phone. "Hi," she said.

"Hi yourself," she heard.

She frowned. It was Larry Cage.

54

Chapter Eight

When he was twelve years old, Gabriel Aubé fell ten feet from the top of a concrete embankment on the Erie Canal, twenty miles from Elmira, New York, and split his head open. His brother, Rayfield, playing with him at the time, carried Gabriel home and, because there was no money for a doctor, or for hospitalization, a deathwatch was begun.

Gabriel's mother was a beautiful, ebony-colored Jamaican who had been coaxed from her homeland fifteen years earlier by a fast-talking and very horny white merchant marine who had abandoned her and his sons several years before Gabriel's accident.

Gabriel's mother did what she could for Gabriel. She cleaned his wound, which was very deep, and which bled profusely, bandaged his head with boiled dish towels, put him in his bed, mopped his brow. And she read to him. She read Byron, and Keats, and Shelley. She read:

> *"Good-night?*
> *Ah! no, the hour is ill*
> *Which severs those it should unite;*
> *Let us remain together still,*
> *Then it will be* good *night."*

And she read:

> *"Swiftly walk o'er the western wave,*
> *Spirit of Night!*
> *Out of the misty eastern cave*
> *Where, all the long and lone daylight,*
> *Thou wovest dreams of joy and fear,*
> *Which makes thee terrible and dear,—*
> *Swift by thy flight."*

And she read:

> *"I weep for Adonais—he is dead!*
> *O weep for Adonais! though our tears*
> *Thaw not the frost which binds so dear a*
>   *head!"*

She had been reading periodically to him from Byron, Keats, and Shelley ever since he was an infant, and he had always listened very intently, not so much because he liked the words he was hearing, but because his mother was speaking them, and as far as Gabriel was concerned, she was creation itself. So, on the day of the accident that necessitated the deathwatch, he had all the words and lines and inflections of several hundred poems stored in his head, and he could recite them at will, though their meanings were obscure to him.

And deep within him, as he lay quietly on what his mother and his brother were mournfully certain was his deathbed, he heard her and he reached frantically for her, because he found in her and in her words and her poetry the strength he desperately needed to cling to life. And cling he did, with great tenacity, while, within his brain, certain vital areas were being denied nourishment, and were dying.

His eyes opened on the fifth day of the deathwatch. They stayed open a full five minutes. Then they closed again, and his mother wept over him and continued reading poetry to him. And waited.

On the seventh day, his eyes opened once more. And stayed open.

"Gabriel?" his mother whispered, disbelieving. Gabriel blinked. "Gabriel?" his mother said again, daring now to hope a little. Gabriel blinked. "Come back to us, Gabriel." He turned his head slowly toward her. A little smile appeared on his lips. His mother wept. His brother wept.

And Gabriel said:

"Much have I traveled in the realms of gold
And many goodly states and kingdoms seen;
Round many western islands have I been
Which bards in fealty to Apollo hold."

And he closed his eyes again, and slept. While certain vital areas of his young brain continued to die.

On the ninth day after the accident, Gabriel sat up suddenly. His mouth dropped open, his eyes fluttered, his arms twitched. Then he lay down again. And he murmured:

"My heart aches, and a drowsy numbness
*   pains*
My sense, as though of hemlock I had drunk,
Or emptied some dull opiate to the drains."

Then he was asleep again.
On the tenth day, he woke once more, sat up,

opened his eyes, and looked hungrily at a bowl
of oatmeal that his brother, Rayfield, was eating.

"Art thou pale for weariness . . ." Gabriel said.

His brother dropped the bowl of oatmeal, ran
over, took Gabriel by the shoulders, and cried,
"Mother, wake up!" because she had fallen
asleep on the crude floor beside the deathbed.
His mother woke instantly and saw that Gabriel
was sitting up. "Oh, my Gabriel, my boy!" she
said to him. And Gabriel said to her, in a voice
that was full and robust, and therefore very sur-
prising:

> *"I fear thy kisses, gentle maiden*
> *Thou needest not fear mine;*
> *My spirit is too deeply laden*
> *Ever to burden thine."*

And he got out of bed, went over to where
Rayfield had dropped the bowl of oatmeal,
picked up the shattered pieces of the bowl—
which still had cereal clinging to them—and began licking them clean, while his mother and
brother watched, half in joy and half in shock,
because they hardly recognized this creature.

He looked blankly at them every few moments
as he ate. *"I fear thy mien, thy tones, thy mo-
tion,"* he said during one of these moments, and,

in another, *"Thou needest not fear mine."*

There were several areas of his brain that still worked. His motor functions were intact, and he could speak, of course. His sight was excellent, too, as were all his other senses. But he could not reason, beyond the very primitive abilities that told him that fire was hot and that winters were cold, so he could not respond. He could react, but he could not respond.

He reacted in the only way that his brain was able to react, using the only means it had salvaged for itself from its own wreckage. He reacted with lines from Keats, Byron, and Shelley. Whatever floated up to the front of his consciousness—like the messages in a Magic 8 Ball—spilled out.

His mother remarried two years later. Another white man. Another mistake. The family moved to Orchid Street, where they lived until tragedy destroyed the street ten years later.

Chapter Nine

"Why would I want to talk to you, Larry?" Katherine said into the phone, then hurried on, "No, no, I didn't ask that. I don't want to listen to what you've got to say, and I know you've probably got a lot to say, you always do—"

"I love you," he cut in.

"That's crap!" She could feel her anger building. "You *love* me? That's crap, and I don't want to hear it because it makes absolutely no difference to anything that's—"

"Love doesn't make a difference, Katherine? Do you really believe that?"

"I don't want to *hear* it, Larry!" She was close to screaming, now. She took a breath, then went on, in a tone of quivering, forced calm, "I do not want to hear anything from you. I've had time, lots of time—"

"You're not going to answer my question?"

"What question?"

"About love." His voice was dripping with sincerity. "About love," he repeated. "Because it for sure means something to me. I had assumed—maybe I was assuming too much—that it meant something to you, too. Sure we've had our ups and downs. Sure I've been a little . . . possessive from time to time, I'm not going to deny it—it's a function of how I feel about you." He paused. In her mind's eye, she could see him smiling, as he always did when they argued. He added, "It's simply a function of my love for you."

"You're trying to manipulate me, Larry. I won't allow it."

"Manipulate you?" He seemed stunned. "Is that what you think I've been doing these past two and a half years, Katherine? Manipulating you? Good Christ!"

"I didn't say anything about the past two and a half years," she told him. "That's *your* guilt trip."

"Oh, for God's sake!" He sounded completely exasperated. "Where are we going with this? Tell me, please, where are we going with this?"

"Larry"—she tried, with her tone, to return his exasperation—"it's over, let's please just—"

"A deal first?" he cut in.

"A deal? What deal?"

"That you answer my question."

She sighed. Her anger had cooled; now she was feeling something closer to exhaustion. "Yes," she said, "of course love means something to me." She said it without conviction. "Okay? Is that what you wanted to hear?"

"Yes," he said. "But only if you mean it. Do you mean it?"

"I mean everything I say, Larry."

"And when you told me you loved me—just a few weeks ago, Katherine—did you mean that? Or was it a lie?"

She said nothing. She didn't know how to answer him. She wanted to tell him that "a few weeks ago" she simply wasn't the person that she was now; she'd been someone else, someone living a life that she despised, now.

He said, "Don't I deserve an answer, Katherine?"

She sighed again. "Yes, I meant it."

"And yet . . . and yet, you're willing to forget I ever existed—"

"Of course not." She felt her eyes watering; it surprised her. "Of course not," she repeated.

"Are you crying?" he asked.

She was about to. "No," she answered.

"I don't like it when you cry, Katherine. Please don't cry."

"Bastard!" she hissed, and in her mind's eye, she saw his smile broaden.

"Yes," he said earnestly, "I admit that—"

"Larry, I'm going to hang up now."

"No, I don't think so. Maybe you *want* to hang up, maybe you think you're *going* to hang up, but you and I both know you aren't going to."

"It's over, Larry, it really is over. I'm through being manipulated—"

"There's that damned word again. You're not being fair, Katherine. We manipulate each other. We have to. It's part of any healthy relationship."

"I don't accept that," she said.

"Of course you do. Of course you do. We have to live for ourselves as much as we live for anyone else. We *have* to be bastards, we *have* to manipulate—and we have to allow ourselves to be manipulated—simply to survive."

"I'm going to hang up now."

"Yes, I believe you are. But keep this in mind—"

"Good-bye, Larry." She took the receiver away from her ear. She heard him shout, "If there really is nothing left between us, then why have we been talking for so damned long?"

She hung up.

* * *

It was late evening and she was lying naked on her back in bed, the top sheet pulled up to her waist and her arms straight at her sides. She was mentally replaying her telephone conversation with Larry, picking out the weak spots, devising snappy replies: "Because I'm civilized, Larry," she whispered, "that's why we talked for so long."

She thought it was very much like him to wreck her first full day at the house—the talk with the boy running, the bit of whimsical planning in the garden, the discovery of the little toolshed, having the phone hooked up. Not a bad first day, *her* day, at least. Not hers and Larry's. There had been too many of those kinds of days.

"*My* day, Larry," she whispered into the darkness, and it occurred to her, painfully, that she wished he were there, in the bed with her, to hear what she was saying. "And *my* house," she finished. It was a wonderfully satisfying thought, so satisfying that it chased the living ghost of Larry away.

She realized that she had had no dinner, that she was ravenous. She threw the top sheet off, sat up—*Hey, what are you doing there, sis?—Putting on a show for the townies?* "Damn you, Jason!" she whispered. She fished a red knee-length cotton robe from a chair nearby, switched on a small Tensor lamp near the bed, noted how little it did to shove back the darkness, and suddenly felt very alone in the house. Alone, vulnerable, and afraid. She cast about in her brain for a reason she was feeling this way, and the reason she found was simplicity itself:

She *was* alone in the house.

And *it* was alone. On its twenty-eight acres.

From below, she heard the phone ringing.

Chapter Ten

1931

"He don't like it in there, Ma," the boy protested. He was twelve years old, soon to be thirteen, tall, thin, and scruffy looking in baggy brown pants, what remained of a dingy white T-shirt, and a red baseball cap with the letters NY imprinted on it in blue. He was barefoot. In the last year and a half, his feet had grown incredibly fast, making it necessary for him to wear custom-made shoes. But his family was dirt-poor and there was no money for custom-made shoes, only a pair of hand-me-down black wing tips that fit badly and made his huge feet hurt, so he rarely wore them. It was for that reason that his mother was punishing him.

She said, "What you mean 'he,' boy?"

"I mean Lazarus, Ma," the boy answered. Lazarus was his special playmate.

She sighed hard. "I gotta tell you this again, don't I? There ain't no Lazarus, and you ain't five years old no more, neither."

The boy said, "He told me it's too hot in there, and he don't like the spiders or the dark, and he don't like—"

His mother slapped him. She was a short, stocky woman—shorter than her son, but far heavier—with a massive square head, shoulder-length, thinning dark brown hair, and tiny, moist, gray eyes that seemed not to move much, as if the muscles were useless, and the only way she could track movement was to move her entire head. Sometimes, people newly introduced to her thought she was blind.

She slapped her son again, for good measure. He stood very still; he'd grown accustomed to her quick temper, and when he had to be around her, he lived in a constant state of stiffened readiness. He asked her, "How long we gotta stay in there this time, Ma?"

She looked stunned. "How long? Till I *say* you can come out. Might be a couple hours, I don't know—might be a couple of days, I don't know." She grinned; he knew that she enjoyed making him nervous. "Or it might be till next month, or the month after that, till I think you learned that civilized people don't go round in bare feet. We ain't white trash, we for damned sure ain't white trash, Galen,"—which was his given name, though she rarely called him anything but "boy"; when she did use his name, he knew she was talking very seriously indeed—"and when you go walking around in your godforsaken big bare feet, well then, it makes the whole family look awful bad."

"Those shoes hurt, Ma. They hurt like the dickens."

Again, she slapped him, much harder than the first two times, so he stumbled backward, into the icebox; he heard something fall over inside it. She rushed over, pushed him to one side, threw the icebox door open, peered in, "Son-bitch!" she muttered. "You broke the son-bitching milk, boy! You broke the son-bitching milk! You know how much we pay for that milk? You know much it costs us to have it delivered here every morning?"

He leaned forward, peered into the icebox, saw that the bottle was lying, unbroken, on its side. "It ain't broke, Ma. See?" he told her. She slammed the icebox door shut, grabbed him by the collar, and dragged him to the back door, into the shallow, weed-choked backyard, where she pointed stiffly, still holding his collar, at a little wooden shed not far off. "Go on, now!" she ordered, and let go of his collar. He didn't obey at once, though his obedience was usually instantaneous. It was such a sweltering hot day, the backyard was infested with bluebottle flies, there was a huge wasp's nest on the outside of the shed, under the roof edge, and he was violently afraid of wasps; he nodded meaningfully at the nest. "They're gonna sting me up till I look like I'm dead, Ma," he whined.

"You don't bother them," she said, and pushed him forward, "and they won't bother you."

He stopped halfway to the shed, looked back. "Please!" he implored. "Lazarus is feelin' kinda sick."

She came forward quickly and pushed at him again. He moved with desperate reluctance to the shed's only door; his mother said, "Lazarus is feelin' sick, huh?" reached around him, and opened the door. "If that's so, then you can keep him company." And she pushed him into the shed. He stood just inside it, very stiffly, his back to her, while a pair of wasps moved sullenly around him, then landed on the coal-dust-streaked pane of warped glass that was the shed's only window. "They'll sting me up real bad, Ma," he pleaded. "They'll kill me and Lazarus for sure."

But she didn't hear him because his voice had grown low and hoarse from fear. She closed the door, threw the bolt that locked it from the outside, and went back into the house to prepare dinner for her husband, who was due home in an hour from his job as a cannery worker at the Duffy-Mott baby food factory. He'd ask where Galen was and when she told him, he'd give her a little argument, and then maybe he'd let Galen out of the shed, and maybe he wouldn't. It depended on what kind of day he'd had.

Galen backed into a corner of the shed, wrapped himself in his arms, despite the incredible heat, and stared wide-eyed at the two wasps meandering about on the window. He heard Lazarus say to him, "I'm feelin' sick, Galen. I'm feelin' awful sick." And he said to Lazarus, "You puke and it'll just stink to high heavens in here!" which he knew to be true from his last time in the shed, a week earlier, when Lazarus had puked a stomachful of bad eggs all over the floor. The shed still smelled of it, though Galen's mother had made him scrub the floor again and again.

One of the wasps took flight, soared toward Galen, and landed on the wall near his shoulder.

A small frightened screech erupted from him, he moved quickly to his left, away from the wasp, and saw out of the corner of his eye that something was on the other side of the shed's miserable little window. He turned his head, looked, but saw little because of the coal dust. He wondered if it was his father, come to let him out. "Dad?" he whispered. A hand came up, wiped away some of the coal dust. A face appeared. Galen saw that it was Gabriel Aubé, Galen closed his eyes and sank to the narrow bench built into the far wall of the shed. It was no use talking to Gabriel, he knew.

He heard dimly, through the window:

"Art thou pale for weariness
Of climbing heaven and gazing on the earth,
Wandering companionless
Among the stars that have a different birth—
And ever changing, like a joyless eye—"

He said, "I'm gonna cry, Lazarus." And Lazarus said to him, "She wants you to cry, Galen." "I know," he said.

And from outside the window, Gabriel said:

"Tell me, thou star, whose wings of light
Speed thee in thy fiery flight,

72

*In what cavern of the night
Will thy pinions close now?"*

Then Gabriel was gone.

In a tumbledown white, Cape Cod–style house on Orchid Street, Matthew Ungen, seventy-eight years old and a widower for nearly a decade, was cursing the city utility for what he considered an unjustifiably high service bill—$3.50 electric— and the coal company, too—$5.00 for a new delivery. He understood the electric bill (hell, he thought, he kept the radio on for half the day), but he didn't understand why he kept using so much coal. Sure he had a coal-fired water heater, and a coal-fired cooking stove, but there was no way he'd used five dollars' worth in the past couple of weeks. He knew that because he washed his dishes in lukewarm water, and then not very often, and he took baths only when he began to itch. So he was angry.

But he'd show them! He'd stop using their damned coal. There were other ways to heat water, and there were other ways to cook meals. Gasoline warmed his car up in the winter, didn't it? It could warm up his house, too, and it could cook his food.

73

Chapter Eleven

"Tell me your name, please," said the voice on · the other end of the line. Katherine didn't recognize it; it sounded like a man's voice, though it could almost as easily have been a woman's, she thought.

She said testily, "Do you know what time it is?"

"Yes, I do," said the voice, and repeated, with emphasis, "Tell me your *name*, please."

Katherine grinned; she could play this stupid game, too. "Perhaps you could tell me yours," she said, and heard a small harrumph of displeasure, followed by a click, and then a dial tone. She stared bemusedly at the receiver, then set it down, whispered a curse at whoever the caller had been, and set about finding something to eat.

She quickly discovered that, except for half a dozen eggs—and she didn't feel like eggs—plus some oatmeal, and the remaining English muffins that Jason had brought, she had no food in the house. She pouted. She knew that until she got some food into her stomach, she wouldn't be able to sleep, especially since her conversation with Larry was still running around in her head.

She went back to the phone—it was on the wall near the kitchen doorway—picked up the Genesee County phone book from the counter, and looked in the scant yellow pages under *P* for *Pizza.* She found only one listing—*Henry's Pizza and Subs To Go,* but it was in Silver Lake, ten miles north, and it was open only until 11:00, so it had closed over an hour earlier. She set the phone book down, considered, picked it up again, looked under *R* for *Restaurants,* found almost a dozen listed, and one, the Hangover Inn, in Honeoye, open twenty-four hours.

She went upstairs, dressed in a pair of jeans, a white blouse, and sneakers, and went out to her car, where she sat quietly, windows open, and let Larry move to her from out of the night. She saw him smile his charming and disarming smile, hands stuck casually into his pants pockets, gait slow but assured. He really was the archetypal cocksure bastard.

He leaned over, looked into the car. "Going somewhere, Katherine?"

76

"Yes," she said, "I'm hungry."

His smile broadened. "And we both know for what, don't we?"

She shook her head briskly. "No," she told him, "you're wrong."

He whispered, "Not about that, Katherine."

She turned her head and stared into his large green eyes. "You bastard!" she hissed, and repeated it, louder; "You bastard!" And she realized that it was not Larry's eyes she was looking into; a little gasp of surprise came from her.

"I'm sorry," the man said. "Did I frighten you?"

She saw the soft glint of a badge. "No . . . yes. . . ." Her breathing became quick and shallow. "You . . . surprised me. Yes."

"Of course I did," the man said, and she saw that his face was round and weathered, pleasant to look at. She explained, "I was going to go out and get something to eat."

"At the Hangover Inn?" the man asked. "It's closed."

"But the phone book says—"

"It closed a month ago. The county health department closed it down."

"I see. . . ."

"The only other all-night place is outside Silver Lake, and that's a twenty-five-mile drive." He paused, then went on, "You're the new owner here, you're Miss Nichols?"

Katherine nodded. "Yes. I moved in today, yesterday, actually."

The man stuck his hand into the car. "I'm Sam Busher; pleased to meet you." Katherine took his hand, though her arm was at an awkward angle. "Yes," she said, "me too. You're the sheriff?"

"Deputy sheriff." He pulled a piece of paper from his pocket, a flashlight from his belt. "I was going to come over about this tomorrow, Miss Nichols—" He shone the flashlight on the piece of paper. "But since you're . . ." He paused a moment, then went on, "Do you know anyone that drives a maroon-colored Mustang, license number—"

"Yes, that's my brother's car, but—"

"And his name is?"

"Jason."

"Is he staying here with you?"

"No. He's not staying here. His car broke down last night. . . ."

"Busted axle, actually. We've got the car in Honeoye."

"I know that. I mean, I know it was a busted axle. He left here to go and find a phone early this morning, a little after eleven-thirty, I think."

"He left on foot?"

"Yes. He was going to try and find that farm—"

"Haislip's farm?"

"I suppose that's what it's called." She remembered Straub's boy had called it that. "Yes, Haislip's farm." She nodded toward the house. "He went around in back of the house, toward the woods—"

The deputy shook his head. "No," he said, "Haislip's farm is south."

"*He* didn't know that." She was losing patience. "He was going to try and find a phone, he was going to call a garage."

"That was this morning?"

"Yes," she answered. "Yes. A little past eleven-thirty, as I said."

"Would you like to file a missing person report, Miss Nichols?"

The question took her by surprise. "No. Of course not." She put her hand on the car's door handle, hesitated, thinking the deputy knew her intentions, opened the door gently into the deputy's knee; he backed away. She got out of the car, shut the door, started for the house.

"Miss Nichols?" the deputy called after her.

She turned toward him. After a moment, she said, "He might have called me?"

"Your brother?"

"I don't know. I don't think so. It could have been—No, I don't think so. It was a crank call. I don't know, it could have been Jason."

"He makes crank calls?"

"No, of course not. He used to, when we were kids." A little quiver of unease went through her.

"Yes," the deputy said, "I see."

"I don't think you do." She wondered why she had suddenly put herself on the defensive; she decided that she didn't like this man, despite his round and pleasant face. He seemed inept, not very bright. "Do I have to go into town?" she asked.

"For what, Miss Nichols?"

"To file a missing person report."

"Oh. No, I don't think so. I'll get all the . . . relevant information . . ." He came forward, pulled a pad and pencil from his shirt pocket, gestured toward the house. "Let's go inside, okay?"

They walked to the house, up the porch steps. She stopped. "He's probably in Honeoye now, wouldn't you say?"

"Quite possibly."

She frowned a little, aware he was humoring her. She opened the front door partway, gestured toward the inside of the house. The deputy took a step toward the door, and Katherine asked, studying his face in the porch light, "What were you doing out here?"

He looked confusedly at her. "You mean in front of your house?"

"Yes." She held the door handle; the door still was open just halfway.

"It's part of my patrol route, Miss Nichols. I come out here a couple of times a week." He kept his friendly blue eyes on her, as if anticipating another question.

"What's there to patrol?" she asked.

He smiled. "I don't understand."

"Out here," she explained. "What's there to patrol? I mean, before I moved in, this was just an empty house, right?"

"Yes." He kept smiling; that unnerved her. "I was patrolling for vandals."

"Vandals? Out in the middle of nowhere?" *People are just as crazy out here,* she remembered Jason telling her, *as they are in the city—there are just fewer of them.* "You must be kidding."

"No, Miss Nichols, I'm not kidding. We have our share of trouble." He continued smiling.

She looked away, pushed the door open wide. "Let's go in," she said. "I'll fill out that report."

He stepped into the house, reached to his right, flicked on the light in the foyer. Katherine looked at him, confused. "Have you been here before?" she asked.

"Yes," he answered. "To look into Mrs. Gore's death." And he went directly into the kitchen. Katherine followed.

Chapter Twelve

1931

Antonio Marchetti, nine, and his sister, Maria, four, spoke no English. They were recent immigrants who, with their mother, Christina, had been established in a simple house on Orchid Street by a man who obtained employment for Christina in the same Duffy-Mott plant were Galen's father worked. He also saw to it that she attended night classes in English, American history, and citizenship at the local high school. He was a man who preferred to remain anonymous, because his philanthropy touched many people and he knew that if his identity were known he'd be swamped with countless thank-yous and would have little time or patience to deal with them.

Christina trusted her son implicitly to care for

his little sister. She had no choice, of course, because there was no money for baby-sitters, so Antonio had been taught how to cook, and to clean up, and to make the little house secure at night. He was a bright and capable boy, but he had lived in an almost constant state of low smoldering anxiety since coming to America six months earlier, so he tended to make mistakes now and again.

During the day, while their mother worked at the Duffy-Mott baby food plant, Antonio and Maria busied themselves with games—hide-and-seek was their favorite—and with eating and nap-taking. They rarely left the house, except with their mother on Sundays to go to church, and occasionally to go to the farmers' market to buy a chicken, which they put—alive—in the cellar for a day or two, until it was ready for slaughter. An icebox had come with the house, but ice was expensive, so Christina did not use it.

On hot midsummer evenings, when sleeping in the poorly ventilated upstairs bedroom was unbearable, Antonio and Maria took their bedding into the cellar, where it was always much cooler and less humid, and where sleep came quickly to them.

It was a small cellar, but Christina kept it scrupulously clean. She had even brought down a spare white wicker chair, a hemp rug, and a floor-standing lamp she'd found in a dump just off Orchid Street, so her children would feel more comfortable. She, too, often slept in the cellar, using the hemp rug and her grandmother's handmade green-and-white-checkered comforter as bedding.

On the evening of August 3, at just past 8:30, on the way home from her evening classes in English and citizenship, Christina turned onto Orchid Street and stopped at once. A small tremor of fear went through her. Something was wrong here, she knew, and she glanced nervously about. Orchid Street was short, and straight, but it was poorly lit. In the midsummer evening dusk, the street's houses—small, carpenter-designed wood-frame dwellings in various stages of repair, except for Gloria's huge Victorian monstrosity— seemed to flow together into a dark red mass of horizontal and vertical lines, windows, porches, and chimneys. A thin layer of coal dust from woodstoves and water heaters hung in the air as well, adding a grimy patina to everything; it made breathing slightly more difficult than it should have been.

It was an early 1930s working-class street in a midsized, northeastern industrial city.

And something was loose on it. Something malevolent. Something that hurt.

Something Christina sensed, now, as surely as she sensed the bad air.

Something Galen also had sensed, from time to time.

And Gloria, too.

And Llewellyn Simms, and Matthew Ungen.

And even Gabriel Aubé, who reacted to it with three lines from a Byron poem."

It was something none of them could ever have hoped to explain or understand. It was something that dwelt within a man who dwelt within a house on Orchid Street.

Christina's gaze took in the whole of the street, but it was difficult for her to see her own house on it, nearly lost, as it was, in the darkness and anonymity of two dozen similar houses.

She was a short, black-haired woman, with smooth, dark Mediterranean features, and exquisite brown eyes. She made her way to her house, now, in short, quick steps, her head down—as if against the cold, although the evening was very warm—and her arms crossed tightly in front of her. She walked in the street itself, because the sidewalk was narrow, pitted, and unpredictable in the darkness. And she walked with a purpose, her mind on her children and their protection.

Some lights were burning in the houses clustered close around her, and she glanced at them now and then. She saw a set of old lace curtains move sullenly in the whisper of a breeze that came up and died. She saw someone's dark profile appear and disappear rhythmically at the edge of another window, as if a rocking chair had been put there, and someone was rocking in it. And she saw another window black out. Not as if the light had been turned off, but as if someone had stepped in front of it. She stopped walking. She heard someone whistling a tune she did not recognize, because the only music she was familiar with was Italian. And then she saw a figure standing in the deep red darkness, and she said to it, in her native tongue, "Who are you?" She remembered, then, what her English instructor had told her, that she was in a land where English was the language people spoke. It was the "American language," he had told her, and so she corrected herself and said in English, "Who are you?"

And a voice came out of the form standing in darkness. It could have been a man's voice, Christina thought. And it could have been a woman's. It said, in Italian, "What is your name, please?"

Christina knew much about respect. She expected it from her children, just as she had been expected to give it to her own parents. And she gave it to everyone else—to older people, to people in authority, and especially to men, because she had been taught that they were her betters. And so, although she did not answer the figure's question at once, because she was frightened, she at last did say, "Christina Marchetti," and added, in a small voice, "My name is Christina Marchetti."

The form stepped forward. It stopped a few feet away and Christina saw in it the suggestion of eyes in a long and narrow face, the suggestion of hands reaching out to her, the suggestion of a smile that was too broad, and too openmouthed. "I love you, Christina Marchetti," she heard.

She said again, with urgency, in her own language, "Who are you?"

And the form repeated what it had just said, though now in Italian, very fluidly, and without accent, "*Ti amo*, Christina Marchetti."

And it took another step forward. Christina became aware of the odor of cloves, and of the faint, stinging odor of starch; she could see that the figure's clothes were dark, formal, and well pressed, and she felt its hands on her hands. She stepped away, with caution, as if the figure were a vicious dog that *wanted* her to run, and she whispered, in Italian, "Who are you?"

She felt its hands on her hands again, on her arms, too, then around her, so its hands were flat on her back, and the odor of its clothing was very strong.

"Who are you?" she said again. "Who are you, please, who are you?"

"*Ti amo,* Christina Marchetti."

She felt its hand flat on the back of her head. She felt her face being pushed into its chest. And its hand was incredibly strong, its chest was layered with cloth, and within minutes, her breathing stopped forever.

Chapter Thirteen

The deputy sat in one of Katherine's new wooden kitchen chairs, pulled a pad and pencil from his jacket pocket, and said, "Your brother's full name, please."

Katherine said, "Jason Andrew Nichols," and spelled it.

"His age?"

"Twenty-eight, just last month." She was in a chair on the other side of the small table. "You probably get lots of people missing up here, don't you?"

The deputy shrugged. "A few. Two or three a year."

Katherine made a small gesture with her hand. "And they probably all turn up after a while, right?"

"Most do, sure. Would you have a recent photograph of your brother, Miss Nichols?"

"Most of them?"

"Sorry?"

"Do you mean that there are some people still missing?"

"Sure. Maybe half a dozen or so in the last thirty years." He paused, then asked again, "Would you have a recent photograph of your brother?"

She ignored him. "What do you think happened to those people?"

He shrugged. "What happens to anyone who just wanders off? People turn up missing every day. Thousands of people every year, I think, and I guess most of them get found eventually. Some don't." He grinned. "But as to what happens to them"—another shrug—"I got no idea."

"What about the people you do find?"

"They'd be hunters, mostly." His tone betrayed his impatience. "People who come down here from the city—weekend hunters, you know, and most of them don't know their asses from a hole in the ground—" A brief pause, an apology, and then he asked again, "Would you have a recent picture of your brother, Miss Nichols?"

She remembered suddenly that he'd asked the question several times. "Oh, yes, I'm sorry. I think I do." She stood. "In the living room. Excuse me. I have a . . . snapshot of him." She left the kitchen, went into the living room, became aware that the deputy had followed her, and was standing in the doorway. "More than a snapshot, really," she told him, and glanced around at the narrow mantel above the fireplace, unsure what she'd done with the photograph. She saw that the mantel was empty. She looked at the deputy. "It's a black-and-white portrait. My own work. I had it enlarged, and framed—" She gave him a quick, quivering grin. "I'm sort of an amateur photographer; I don't do my own developing, of course."

"I thought you were an artist, Miss Nichols."

"Yes, I am." She became aware that he was making her feel ill at ease, and she wasn't sure why. She thought for a moment that it was because he was the first man, other than Jason, to be inside the house with her, but discarded the idea at once because it was so obviously silly and schoolgirlish, and because it hinted at the kind of stiff, puritanical attitudes the religious cult had tried to instill in her. She went on, "But you should realize, Mr. Busher, that photography is a genuine art form."

He shrugged. "Who can tell?" he said, and nodded at something behind her. "Is that the picture you're talking about?"

She looked. "Where?" she said, and looked

where he'd nodded. Strange, she thought; she couldn't remember putting Jason's portrait on the walnut table under the far window, where it sat now. She couldn't remember, in fact, even unpacking it.

"There," the deputy answered, stood, crossed to the table, picked up the portrait, studied it a moment, then brought it back to her. "Is this your brother?"

"Yes," she said, "that's Jason."

"Can I take this with me?"

She glanced at the walnut table, still confused, then looked at the deputy again. "Yes," she said, "you can take it."

"Would you say that this is a true likeness of your brother, Miss Nichols?"

"A true likeness?"

"Has he grown a beard or a mustache since this was taken?"

"No. He's clean-shaven." She looked again at the table, kept her gaze on it. "Except for a little mustache; he's just started it."

The deputy asked, "Something wrong, miss?"

She didn't answer. She was thinking that not only did she not remember putting Jason's portrait on the table, she didn't remember the table, either.

"Miss Nichols?" the deputy coaxed, and put

his hand on her shoulder to get her attention.

She turned her head and gave him a small, confused smile. "No," she said, "nothing's wrong. I think I'm tired. It's late."

The deputy let his hand drop. She watched it drop, watched it clench into a fist, then loosen, as if he were stretching it. She asked, still looking at it, "Do you think he's all right?" She looked into the deputy's face.

"I expect so," he answered, then looked away, as if not wanting to hold her gaze. "People usually show up before long." He looked back, asked her a couple more questions—again about when she'd last seen Jason, and where, exactly, he was then, and if he had any medical problems: "Asthma, diabetes, a heart condition, that sort of thing," he said.

To which she answered, "As far as I know, Jason's in excellent health." And after a few pleasantries and unconvincing reassurances, the deputy left the house.

Chapter Fourteen

1931

At not quite 10:00 in the evening, Galen awoke in the little wooden gardening shed that his mother had put him in as punishment for going barefoot. He woke with a pain in the back of his neck and back from trying to sleep on the hard, narrow bench, and he woke layered with sweat because the shed had been gathering the summer heat all day long and now would not let it go.

Galen was strong and wiry. He knew that without much effort he could force the shed door open. But that fact was unimportant to him. His mother had put him here, and this was where he had to stay. To defy her once was stupid, but to defy her twice was insanity.

Galen sat up on the bench and held his arms out wide so that some of his sweat might evap-

orate, but it did little good because the air in the
shed was motionless and palpably humid. He
pulled his shirt off, stood, and took the few steps
over to the shed's miserable window. In the cen-
ter of this window the grime had been wiped
away—by poor Gabriel Aubé, early in the
afternoon, he remembered—and he peered
through at his house. He saw that several lights
were burning; one downstairs, one upstairs—in
his bedroom, at the back of the house—and in
the bathroom. Galen wondered about this. Elec-
tricity was expensive, and his mother never kept
lights on unless it was absolutely necessary. He
couldn't remember a time when more than two
lights had been kept burning at night.

Between the shed and the house, the yard was
thickly overgrown with weeds, although, over
the years, Galen's mother had worn a small path
from the house to the shed, bringing him to it as
punishment. Sometimes she brought him to the
shed five or six times a week.

Galen said now, turning his head to look at
the narrow bench, "Lazarus, they've got a lot of
lights on in the house." And he watched as Lazarus—Galen's age and height, but even leaner
and scruffier looking, with a mass of dirty, coal-
black hair that wormed down over his shoulders,
a constant, five-day growth of a twelve-year-old's

beard, and coal-black eyes that seemed to hold a constant look of terror in them—pushed himself up off the bench, precisely where Galen had been sleeping, came over, and stood shoulder to shoulder with Galen.

He looked at the house for a full minute, and then he said, in a voice that was powerful and confident (because he was outwardly Galen's dismal reflection, but inwardly what Galen had always dreamed of being—strong and heroic), "They'll shut her off if she can't pay." Galen nodded meaningfully. Lazarus went back to the bench, sat down, crossed his legs, clasped his big, bony hands in front of his knees, and let his head rest against the shed wall. He said again, "They'll shut her off if she can't pay." And added, "There'll be no light in that house, then." He unclasped his hands and leaned forward. "I hear something," he said.

And Galen became aware that *he* was hearing something, too. "What is it, Lazarus?"

"Quiet," Lazarus said. "I'm listening."

Galen stayed quiet. Lazarus said, "I hear someone whistling."

Galen nodded. "I hear someone whistling, too."

"I hear someone whistling 'The Foggy, Foggy Dew,' " Lazarus said. "That's what I hear."

"It's what I hear, too, Lazarus."

"Someone right outside there." He nodded at the shed door. "Right outside there."

Galen nodded urgently: "You're right, Lazarus—" He was cut off by a voice—a man's, a woman's; he couldn't be sure—which asked through the door, "What is your name, please?"

Galen did not answer. He pressed the side of his head to the window again. He saw little. He whispered, "I can't see nothin', Lazarus."

And then the figure who had been whistling "The Foggy, Foggy Dew," the figure that had a woman's voice, a man's voice—no one could be sure—unlatched the shed door, pulled it open, and stepped inside very quickly, with much grace, while Galen backed awkwardly away and called, "Lazarus? You there, Lazarus?" But Lazarus wasn't there.

Then the figure who had stepped into the shed said again, "What is your name, please?"

And Galen, wishing very much that he could see something of the figure's face, beyond the mouth that was too wide, answered, "My name is Galen," and then watched as the figure stepped forward and held his arms out. "I love you, Galen."

Galen could not speak. He sensed something powerful here. Something that hurt.

100

And then he recognized the figure, could say its name, and was about to, but couldn't, because his face was suddenly buried in layers of soft cloth over the figure's chest, and the figure's incredibly powerful right hand was holding him motionless, so even the hot, humid air inside the shed could not reach him, and make his lungs swell. And keep him alive.

Chapter Fifteen

When she woke after only a couple of hours of sleep, Katherine was instantly aware of two things: She was aware that Jason was missing, and it was a fact that seemed very strange, and hard to deal with. It was even difficult to define. What did "missing" mean, exactly? It didn't mean "dead," although it could (but then it wouldn't mean "missing" anymore, would it?). It meant . . . nothing. It meant "limbo." Jason was in limbo, no one knew where he was. Except maybe himself. She couldn't call him on the phone—although she'd tried several times after the deputy had left the house. She couldn't leave her little bedroom and go into the other bedroom or downstairs to the living room or kitchen and find him there. He was *missing*. And until he was not missing anymore, she knew that her attention and energy would be riveted to that fact.

She swung her feet to the floor, sat groggily on the edge of the bed, and focused on the other fact she'd been aware of upon waking—that someone was shuffling around on the front porch. She glanced at the alarm clock: 7:15. She called hoarsely, "Who's down there?" but got no answer, although whoever it was surely could have heard her through the open window. She stood, reached out for one of the tall bedposts, steadied herself, let a quick wave of dizziness wash over her. She put her robe on—she kept it at the foot of the bed (*What are you doing, sis? Putting on a show for the townies?*)—went over to the window, put her hands on the sill:

"Who's down there?"

She heard what she had heard once before—early the previous morning, she remembered; she heard the sound of glass gently striking glass.

"Who's *there?*"

The sound continued. It was, she realized, exactly like the soft, tinkling noises that glass bottles make when carried.

"I've got a gun!" she screamed. It was a lie, doubtless a foolish one, too. "And I'm not afraid to use it!"

The noises stopped. The shuffling stopped. She made her way out of the bedroom, down the short, narrow stairway to the first floor, and then into the living room, which was still dark because the curtains were drawn. She stopped several feet from the front door, clenched and unclenched her fists nervously, listened. She heard an engine start, heard it being revved. Then she heard the clanking sound of old gears meshing. She ran to the door, threw it open. She saw that the road in front of the house was empty; a small cloud of dust wafted toward her on a slight morning breeze.

"Could I speak with Deputy Sheriff Busher, please?"

"I'm sorry, he's off duty, ma'am." It was a young woman's voice and it had a distinct country twang to it. "Who's calling?"

"My name's Katherine Nichols. Deputy Busher took a missing person report from me last night and I was wondering if he's turned up anything."

"Turned up anything?"

"On my brother—he's the one who's missing. His name's Jason Nichols." She spelled it.

"You say the deputy took this report last night?"

"Yes. It was late, about twelve."

"Did he take the report here at the station?"

"No." Katherine was trying hard to control her

temper. "He took it here, at my house." She gave the woman her address.

"And this was at about midnight last night, you say?"

"Yes."

"Well, I'm sorry, but Sam hasn't filed it yet. How long has your brother been missing?"

"Since yesterday morning, since Tuesday morning. What do you mean he hasn't filed it yet?"

"What time yesterday, Miss Nichols?"

"Late morning. Eleven, eleven-thirty, I guess. Listen, your deputy has already taken all this information. Don't you think you should give him a call?"

"He's due in at nine-thirty, Miss Nichols. We'll get the report then. In the meantime—"

"You'll get the report *then?* You don't seem to appreciate the fact that my brother is *missing*—"

"Miss Nichols, you have to understand that until twenty-fours has elapsed there's nothing we can do."

"The deputy never told me that."

"Well, he shoulda. He probably did, in fact. Sam's a good man. Goes by the book."

"So, what are you saying to me? Are you saying . . ." She caught her breath, went on more slowly, "Are you saying that I've got to wait around here? Are you saying that you people can't do anything for . . . what? Four hours? Until noon?"

"Or thereabouts, that's right, Miss Nichols. Sorry."

"You can't even send the deputy back out here?"

"He's probably sleeping."

"Is that supposed to concern me? My *brother* is missing, damn it!"

"No need for shouting, Miss Nichols. It won't have no effect on what can or cannot be done. Now, if you think there's some sort of foul play going on with your brother's disappearance—"

"Of course I don't think that." She'd responded too quickly, she realized. "I have no reason to believe that foul play is involved."

"Well then, there's not a lot we can do right now, is there? Listen, why don't I have Sam call you when he gets here, and then he can tell you what he's planning to do? I'm sure he'll get some kind of search going, he always does."

"Always does?"

"Sure, in cases like this. He's a very thorough man, extremely thorough, very much by the book, but you've got to promise to give us a call if your brother shows up. It's possible he's just wandered off—"

"Oh, Christ, Jason is almost thirty years old."

"Oh. I didn't know that, Miss Nichols. Sorry. But please give us a call if he does come back, okay?"

"Can I have the deputy's home phone number?"

"Can't do that. Sorry. It's unlisted."

She sighed. "Okay. Just have him call me. I'll be here." And she hung up.

Chapter Sixteen

1931

He lived alone in a house on Orchid Street that was like most of the houses on the street—a small, nondescript, wood-frame dwelling in an indifferent state of repair.

His parents, who had died of influenza in the same awful week two decades earlier—in a month that saw a dozen other influenza-related deaths on the street—had bequeathed him the house, as well as the care of his infant brother, Samuel. It was a task in which he placed almost religious significance.

Samuel was buried in a small, handmade wooden casket behind the house, near a huge elm tree that was just then beginning to fall victim to the same blight that would sooner or later claim most of the elms in the state. Samuel had a crude rattle made out of a dried gourd clutched in one hand, and a teddy bear in the other; he wore the white cotton pajamas he'd been wearing on the night of his death, and a green blanket had been put on him to keep him warm.

Samuel had been killed by his brother to protect him from one incredibly cold winter night, and the same slow and terrible death that had taken his parents. It had been an easy and comforting death—a long embrace, a few murmured words of love ("I love you, Samuel"), and then a song: "And all that night I held him in my arms, just to keep him from the foggy, foggy dew."

But Samuel's brother no longer sang well. A small, recently developed tumor at the base of his larynx made it painful for him to sing—to reach into his diaphragm and push a volume of air up over that small tumor made what had been a passable, almost pleasing tenor into a miserable low screech. And so he had taken to whistling, which did not require the same muscles, or the same passage of air, and which he did very well.

He was a man of awkward dimensions. His legs were thin and short, his arms very long and powerful, and his hands oversized, with long, thin fingers that would have been the envy of any pianist. His chest was wide and flat, and his face abnormally oblong—the mouth large, lips thin, nose small, and eyes set far apart.

For twenty years, ever since the murder of his infant brother, he had been moving about under duress. If anyone had bothered to ask him about himself, he would have explained that he did only those things that he was directed to do. And if anyone had asked him who directed him to do these things, he would have said that it was the entity that lived inside him, the entity that had no name, or form, or purpose that it could share with him. He would have explained, also, that he was really quite happy living with this entity inside him because it was much easier seeing himself through the long days and longer nights doing only what the entity directed him to do.

But no one ever asked him much about himself—beyond the formalities of everyday life, his name (Hayward Sloat), his age (thirty-six on the night of the fire that destroyed Orchid Street), and his occupation (caretaker). He lived alone inside his little house on Orchid Street. And an entity that he knew nothing about lived inside him. It forced him from his bed in the morning, and into the bathroom, to the breakfast table, to work, and home again.

And, on certain nights, it forced him from the house and onto the street, then into the shadows, where it reached from deep inside him, and moved him, as if he were a marionette, and made him do the things he could not help doing—the things he knew he really did not want to do, but which felt very, very good to do.

Chapter Seventeen

For a day and a half, Katherine helped Deputy Sam Busher and half a dozen townies in the search for her brother. The search involved the fields behind Katherine's house and the stand of woods a half mile off, plus much acreage to either side. Tom Haislip, whose farm Jason had gone in search of, was interviewed as well, and he said that he'd seen someone the morning of the disappearance, but that it had probably been a hunter, that, at any rate, he'd heard rifle fire, but if he turned up anything "vital" to the investigation, he'd call the station.

The skeletal remains of an Irish setter—fur still attached—missing from Willow Point for almost a year were found in the stand of woods, and one of the townies was dispatched to deliver the sad news to the dog's owners. There were other discoveries, too, that might have proved interesting under different circumstances—a boy's baseball cap, circa 1920, the deputy guessed, the hood ornament from an ancient Ford, a badly rusted harmonica, plus some fresh tire tracks halfway between the woods and the house. This discovery upset Katherine because the locals seemed to take such liberties with her property.

Jason's footprints were found, too, along a stretch of mud near a narrow creek that ran along the northern edge of the woods. "Well," the deputy said, "at least we know he got *this* far."

"How do you know they're Jason's?" Katherine asked, and the deputy explained, with exaggerated patience, that hunters wore hunting boots, of course, and that "city people, like your brother, Miss Nichols," did not. They wore crepe-soled shoes. He pointed at the footprints. "Like these here were," he said. And Katherine remembered dimly that Jason did indeed wear crepe-soled shoes. The prints, however, were the only real pieces of evidence that the search party found, and near the middle of the second day, the deputy suggested—with what seemed to Katherine to be a newfound sense of humility—that maybe "the state boys should be brought in, because maybe we got to widen our search pattern just a little."

The head of the Missing Persons Department for the Genesee County Division of the state police was a man in his early fifties, balding, overweight, and more than a bit surly. His name was Kennedy Whelan, and though he held the rank of captain, he much preferred being called Mr. Whelan.

He had a predilection for large and smelly Cuban cigars, so the picture he presented was of a stereotypical country sheriff who chose to dress in dark, three-piece suits, spoke very well, and wanted everyone to stay out of his way because he had a job to do.

He was also gay. This was a fact that had given him no end of psychic torment in his younger years, and which he now hid under a nearly constant stream of macho bullshit. He supposed at times that he might be overdoing the whole act. He wasn't. Most people believed it. He had, in fact, been doing it for so long that he had begun to believe it himself. It would have been very painful for him to learn that even those who professed to be his closest friends thought of him as just another asshole who had too much power.

It's what Katherine thought almost immediately when he swept into her house, followed by a trooper in plainclothes, and one in uniform, flashed his badge, introduced himself, lit up his cigar, fell into a chair that was much too small for him, and demanded, "Can you tell us, Miss Nichols, that you've been straight with the local police?"

Katherine shook her head a little, unsure how to answer.

Whelan leaned forward and poked the air with his cigar. "Can you affirm, Miss Nichols, that you had nothing to do with your brother's disappearance?"

She'd been standing near the entranceway, arms crossed. Whelan's question made her queasy and light-headed. "*Damn* you!" she said.

Whelan said, "Had to ask. Sorry," though his brusque tone said clearly that he wasn't. "Do you think it's possible that your brother just decided to . . . become one of the missing?"

"I don't understand that, either."

"I mean, was he having any problems—with his job, with his women, et cetera, that might have made him decide to—"

"No. He wasn't having any problems that I'm aware of—"

"No problems?" Whelan grinned. "Well then, he'd be unique, wouldn't he?"

116

Katherine shook her head in frustration. "He wasn't suicidal, if that's what you're inferring—"

"I'm *inferring* nothing," Whelan cut in, smiling again. "I'm *implying* that he might have simply decided, for reasons to which only he would be privy, to stage his own disappearance. *You* may infer from that implication whatever you wish."

My English lesson for the day, Katherine thought.

Whelan went on, "People are strange, Miss Nichols. Perhaps you've noticed. People are exceedingly strange. Stranger by far than bats or turkey vultures or Tasmanian devils. And so they do exceedingly strange things." He paused.

Katherine said, "Is there a point to all this, Mr. Whelan?"

"Isn't there always a point?" Whelan said, and added, "What kind of man was your brother?"

Katherine thought a moment, then answered, "A very kind man, a very gentle man. We're quite close." *What are you doing there, sis? Putting on a show for the townies?* "We've always been quite close."

"Did he have any mental problems? Was he under a doctor's care?"

"I'm sorry, I don't know what you mean— mental problems. He was very healthy. Mentally and otherwise."

117

T. M. WRIGHT

Whelan didn't respond at once. The ghost of a smile came and went on his lips, as if he had latched on to something tasty. He glanced at the plainclothes cop, standing near the doorway, looked back at Katherine, said, "You'd know better than I." He leaned forward and studied his cigar as he spoke. "Tell me what you mean when you say that you and your brother were 'very close.' I'm interested in that."

Katherine shook her head, confused.

Whelan said, "If you think there's anything salacious in my interest, you'd be very wrong."

Katherine shook her head again. "We . . . loved each other, as brothers and sisters should—"

"And even more than brothers and sisters should, isn't that right, Miss Nichols?"

She bristled. "No, that isn't right, you bastard!"

Whelan grinned. "Please understand, Miss Nichols, that this house is . . . unique, and it's apparently kept under periodic surveillance—"

"Good Lord, are you telling me that I've been *spied* on?"

"Let's not get melodramatic," Whelan said, and stuck his cigar back into his mouth. "All I'm saying to you is that in the course of the dep-

118

uty's . . . protective surveillance you were seen
with your brother in a clearly compromising position, a position that indicates to me at least that
you and your brother might have had a relationship that could not be defined as normal." He
grinned again, as if savoring his observation.

Katherine came quickly across the room and
slapped him hard across the face, knocking the
fat cigar from his mouth. It fell into his lap,
lighted end down, which burned a hole in his suit
pants and scorched his thigh. He cursed, pushed
the cigar to the hardwood floor, and jumped to
his feet, wide-eyed and shivering with rage. Katherine slapped him again, even harder, but he was
a rock-solid man and his head merely shook
slightly. He grabbed her wrists, pushed her back
into her chair, bent over her. "You fucking lousy
bitch!" he spat, and she turned away because his
breath smelled of stale cigar smoke and coffee.
The uniformed trooper stepped forward; Whelan
turned his head and growled, "I'll handle this!"
The trooper backed off. The plainclothes cop
said, "Don't lose your cool, Kennedy. She's only
a woman."

Whelan ignored him. He turned back to Katherine. "Let me tell you something, cutie . . ."
Katherine was still looking away. "Hey," he

barked, "look at me. I'm *talking* to you." She turned her head back and gave him a blank look that was designed to be disinterest. "Good," he said.

"Let go of my goddamned wrists!" she demanded.

The plainclothes cop said, "Let go of her wrists, Kennedy."

Again, Whelan ignored him. "You know what, cutie? I could bring charges against you for what you just did."

"Let go of my wrists!" Katherine repeated. She was clearly nervous, but very angry, too.

The plainclothes cop said, "Kennedy, please—"

And Whelan let go of her wrists. He straightened over her, hesitated, then made a show of examining the hole in his suit pants. "You'll get a bill," he snarled, then leaned over, retrieved the cigar from the floor—it left a long narrow burn in the wood—and sat down. He stuck the cigar into his mouth and smiled broadly, as if the recent encounter had never happened. "I want to know the truth, Miss Nichols, and I want the truth, now: Did you and your brother—" She shook her head violently, eyes closed. *The lady protests too much!* he thought, and said, his voice louder, more strident, "Did you and your brother have an incestuous relationship?"

She continued shaking her head but looked him squarely in the eye: "No, for God's sake—"

"Are you sure?"

"Am I *sure?*"

The plainclothes cop said, "Kennedy, do you really think that any of this is relevant?"

Whelan gave him a withering gaze. "Of course it's relevant. Murder is a family affair—I'm sure you're aware of that." He smiled again. "And when you've got a little hanky-panky going on besides—"

The cop shrugged. "Let's just make it snappy, okay?" He checked his watch. "I got a couple appointments."

"We'll take whatever time we need, Tom." He looked at Katherine, again. "Did you have an incestuous relationship with your brother, Miss Nichols?"

Katherine forced her anger down. "I am not going to answer that question again, Mr. Whelan. I think it's insulting."

"Of course it is," Whelan said. He pushed himself heavily to his feet. "We're going to be going over the same ground that the deputy and his men have gone over. And if that yields nothing, then we'll expand the search. We'll find your brother, Miss Nichols, I can guarantee it." Then

121

he turned and left the house, followed by the other two cops.

After a moment, Katherine went out onto the front porch. A half dozen state police cars were parked in front of the house, plus several pickup trucks and private cars. A dozen men were clustered around Whelan, who was waving his arm toward the back of the house. Katherine wanted badly to ask him what he'd meant when he had said that her house was "unique." She wanted to know why it had been watched (and so had enabled Busher to see what he'd seen). And she wanted just as badly to deal with him only out of deep necessity, because dealing with him at all made her feel strangely unclean, and very angry. She didn't know precisely at whom.

Chapter Eighteen

1931

Gloria liked being naked. She had no illusions about herself; she did not believe that her incredible obesity was at all pleasant to look at. She didn't even believe that Llewellyn Simms, who painted her once a week, enjoyed looking at her. She liked being naked because there was such great honesty in it, and she was a great believer in honesty.

Llewellyn Simms was late today. He had promised to come by before 12:00 and it was 12:15. It wasn't like him to be late; he was almost compulsively punctual—nervous, yes, and maybe a bit stupid, but always punctual.

Gloria drifted silently about her big sitting room. She had learned to move without making much noise, despite her size, and it was something in which she took pride.

The redbrick Victorian monstrosity she lived in was unique on Orchid Street. It was situated near the northeast end of the street—a small, white wood-frame house, in which Christina Marchetti and her children lived, stood next door, at the corner, where Orchid Street met Jay Street.

Gloria adored her huge, ugly house. She adored having so many rooms in which to move about, because she loved *bigness*. Consequently, she had provided the house with only the barest of furnishings. One chair in the sitting room—a large flower-print Queen Anne chair, and a tall grandfather clock near the far corner (because she liked to keep track of time; she had installed a clock in each of the rooms she used). Light was provided by an ornate brass ceiling fixture. Her bedroom, though as large as most living rooms, contained only her queen-size brass bed, yet another grandfather clock, and a small dresser (she did not often wear clothes).

She also left most of her windows uncovered. They were tall, narrow, Victorian windows and at night, from outside, they gave a wonderful view of the inside of the house, and of the expansive Gloria moving about naked from room to room.

Some of the people on Orchid Street saw this as scandalous, others as a kind of off-key joke. The police had once been summoned, but when they arrived and saw the object of the complaint, they chuckled, made a few caustic remarks, and drove off without confronting Gloria.

She picked a glass of iced tea up from the floor—she drank lots of iced tea in the summer—sipped it delicately, then set the glass down on the floor again. From somewhere else in the big house she heard someone padding about, as if to conceal his movements. She turned her huge body fully toward the sound. "Is someone there?" she called. The noises stopped and she guessed that they had come from the kitchen, which had a wide plank floor that made more noise than the oak floors in the rest of the house.

She moved quickly and silently out of the sitting room and into the hallway that led to the kitchen. She told herself that the person who had been padding about was probably Llewellyn Simms, that he'd come in the back door and was rummaging about in her icebox. But she knew even as she thought it that this was incorrect. Llewellyn ate only when he was very hungry. He had even once confessed to her that for reasons he didn't understand, eating was distasteful to him—"indelicate," he said, then apologized pro-

fusely because Gloria had clearly taken the
remark personally.

"Llewellyn?" she said now, and her voice,
which was normally a very confident, if pinched,
alto, was little more than a high, nervous whisper.

She peered down the hallway into the kitchen.
Afternoon sunlight was streaming in through a
west-facing window; she could see her small,
round wooden table, two sturdy wooden chairs,
her cupboards, voluminous, glass-covered, and
chock-full with canned goods, the front edge of
her mammoth, black iron cooking stove, only recently converted to gas. "Llewellyn?" she said
again, though the noises from within the kitchen
had ceased.

She moved cautiously down the hallway. It
was wide and well lit, and halfway to the kitchen
she became aware of her nakedness, as if someone's disapproving gaze was on her, so she
turned and started back to the sitting room,
where she kept a red housedress. It was when
she turned, and had started walking back, that
she heard from close behind her, "What is your
name, please?"

She did not stop walking. Something deep in
her consciousness had been telling her all along
that someone other than Llewellyn Simms was

126

in the house with her. And now that she heard the voice, she recognized it. She had heard it before, on the street—"Good morning, Gloria." . . . "Good afternoon, Gloria." . . . "Very pleasant day, isn't it?" But there was a small tremor in it, now, as if it were straining against itself, as if the words it had just spoken encompassed real physical pain and anger, as if a dog that had gone rabid had developed a voice and language to communicate its terrible, self-destructive frenzy.

And so she kept walking, because at that moment, she knew for the first time in her life what it was to be afraid.

She heard again, as she walked, "What is your name, please?"

She squeaked, "My name is Gloria," and kept walking. She did not turn and look. And when a hand and an arm fell across her breasts from behind, she expected it, but she cried out nonetheless, "Help me!" though it sounded very weak and stupid to her, even as she screamed it.

She fell. Around her, the floors and walls vibrated madly. She lay on her belly. She was aware of the odors of cloves and starch.

"I love you, Gloria."

She did not thrash about. She couldn't. Inside her massive chest, her poor and panicked heart had been asked to pump far more blood around

127

her huge body than it possibly could, and so it had refused.

"I love you, Gloria."

She thought, then, that there were probably far less pleasant ways to die.

Antonio and Maria Marchetti had waited for their mother to come back from her evening classes in civics and English, and when they had fallen asleep at last—in the cool cellar—they had told themselves that when they woke, their mother would be there, calling them to a breakfast of cornmeal mush and maybe an egg each (a once-a-month treat).

But when Antonio woke and called, "Mama?" but got no answer, he shook his sister. "Get up, Maria!" he said in Italian, and together they went upstairs, where they found that the little house was empty.

They did not go outside. All their young lives their mother had always come back to them. She never left them alone for very long, never more than a full day, and then only once, when she had gone to the Duffy-Mott plant and worked three shifts in a row.

So, they waited. Antonio made a breakfast of cornmeal mush and day-old milk, which was beginning to turn, and afterward he told his sister to wait in the living room, on the couch, with one of her picture books, while he sat waiting on a small bench in the foyer. He had no doubt his mother would return soon. He didn't even question where she might be; that was her concern. But he did miss her, as did Maria.

By 2:30, a picture book opened on her lap, Maria was quietly sobbing. *"Mia madre,"* she whispered over and over again.

Two hundred yards away, behind a nondescript white wood-frame house, the body of Christina Marchetti sat up suddenly in tall weeds. It was no great feat—corpses were known to sit up from time to time. But then, with the sunlight on her, she turned her head and her closed eyes in the direction of her house and her children, and a grief so intense that it penetrated death itself tore through her. And her vocal cords—in the initial stages of decomposition—ripped themselves apart in a quick and tortured scream.

Then she lay down again and was still.

Chapter Nineteen

One week after his disappearance, the search for Jason Nichols officially ended. Kennedy Whelan made clearly insincere apologies and condolences to Katherine, and added, "But keep in mind, please, that no missing person's file is ever really closed. Especially this one," which left Katherine very angry and very sad—a combination that exhausted her.

Two hours later, she called Deputy Sheriff Busher.

"Deputy?" she said, and heard that her voice was quivering.

"Yes, Miss Nichols?"

Silence.

"Miss Nichols?" the deputy coaxed.

"Yes," she said. "Yes." After several moments of silence, Katherine went on, "I got a phone call.

Someone called me. Just fifteen minutes ago."
Again she fell silent.

"Who called you, Miss Nichols?"

She sighed. "I don't know. A man. He
didn't . . ." She took a breath. "He didn't give me
his name."

"What did he say?"

Silence.

"Was it something about your brother? Did
this man say something about your brother?"

"Yes." It was a whisper.

"I'm sorry, Miss Nichols, I didn't hear you,
could you, please . . ."

"Yes," she screamed. "God, yes, it was about
Jason. He said that Jason's dead! He said he shot
him—this man said he shot him, he said he was
hunting and he fired at what he thought was a
deer and he shot Jason. Oh God—" She burst
into a fit of weeping.

"Good Christ," the deputy murmured, and
added soothingly, "Miss Nichols, please, this is
important—"

"He's out there," Katherine cut in, her voice
tinged with disbelief and grief. "This man said
that Jason is out there behind the house."

"*Where*, Miss Nichols? Did this man say where
behind your house?"

"Yes—" Katherine began, and the deputy cut in.

"Stay where you are. I'll be there directly."

Katherine moved leadenly about in her little house while she waited for Busher to appear. Her thoughts were small and pleasant. They flitted about and vanished and then came back, as if wanting to be made clearer, or rearranged, because they were memories from her childhood, of growing up with Jason, and so they were dim memories.

She and Jason had been the only children in the family, he older by four years, and from the start he had been inculcated with the idea that older brothers were expected to be supermen. They were protectors, confidants, sages. They were even better than fathers because they shared a generation with their younger siblings. And because they had quite recently gone through the same torments and tortures of growing up that those siblings were now undergoing, they could be expected to lend a helping hand. It was, overall, an impossible task, Katherine realized now, though a tiny and affectionate smile moved across her lips as she remembered Jason's almost constant attempts to live up to it.

Behind their big country house in Vermont,

for instance, where dozens of neighborhood kids swung Tarzan-style over a deep gully on long, thin vines, Jason always warned her that, yes, she could swing too, but she had to do it holding on to him. "Hang on tight, sis," he told her. That way, he explained, if the vine broke, then his body would cushion her fall. It had always been such a good memory. And *damn* Kennedy Whelan—who knew nothing about it—for making it seem somehow unclean.

And when boys started hanging around her, when, as her father put it, she had begun to "bud nicely," Jason saw to it that no one hung too close. That was a job he seemed to take very seriously, a job he stuck to, in fact, until she went off to college. He never raised a hand to anyone. Never threatened. His presence always seemed to be threat enough. She remembered now that she had begun resenting him around her sixteenth year, and that her resentment no doubt showed. She hoped it hadn't shown too much. She hoped that Jason—who had always been very perceptive and sensitive—saw through her surface resentment to the spot deep within her where her real thankfulness surely dwelled.

Because Jason was dead now. And if he had made mistakes, then it proved only that he was one of five or six billion other human beings on the planet.

Jason was dead now. She could never touch him again, or be kissed by him, or hear his voice.

Damn Kennedy Whelan for dirtying his memory!

Zombies had been fun, too. One of their favorites, especially when they were alone and the other kids who lived nearby were busy with other things. Another good memory. Because as big as he was, Jason had made a great zombie.

And *Tootsie Toes,* too—

So what if he had made mistakes? So what if he'd been possessive of her, maybe too possessive of her? Didn't it prove only that he was just one of five or six billion other human beings . . .

"Damn you!"

She was aware only dimly that she'd said the words, as if it had been a thought that had come to her when she was close to sleep.

Jason is dead now!

That bastard hunter has killed Jason!

"Damn you!" she said again, and in her mind's eye, she conjured up the face of the hunter. It was long, narrow, and unshaven, with close-set, vacant eyes, a nose that had clearly been broken too many times, and thin white lips that did little to hide rotted teeth. It was the very personification of the kind of ignorance and evil that could mistake a tall, well-built, sensitive, and troubled man for a deer.

"Damn you! Goddamn you!"

Her wanderings had taken her into the kitchen, to the back door, where she focused, now, on a set of lights behind the house—the same set of lights she had seen on her first night here, just eight days earlier. They could have been streetlights, she thought, and she heard a knock at the front door. Deputy Sheriff Busher had arrived.

She watched him move stiffly, as if with great agitation, into the house, into the living room, where he stood near the windows fidgeting, his right fist opening and closing over his holstered .45.

"Did you recognize the man's voice, Miss Nichols?" He sounded strained. She decided it was no wonder, because this was a murder case, now.

She answered, in a voice that was also strained and also, she thought, for good reason, "I didn't recognize his voice. It was a man's voice. A middle-aged man's voice, I guess." She was sitting in her white wicker chair only a couple of feet from Busher and she was hunched forward with her elbows on her knees and her hands clasped. She could smell cherry tobacco on him.

He asked, "What did this man say, exactly?"

"He said . . ." She let her thoughts sort themselves out— *Hang on tight, sis! . . . C'mon, sit closer, stay warm! . . . Damn you, goddamn you! . . . What in the hell are you doing? My God*— "He said, 'I'm sorry. I've killed your brother. I shot him.'" She stopped again; her eyes began to tear, memories lumping together like the commingling of bad smells. *Hang on tight, sis, hang on tight! That's right! . . . Damn you! . . . Hang on tight! . . . Giving the townies a show, sis? . . . My God, what are you doing? . . . Hang on tight!* She took a deep breath and went on, "Then he said it again. The same thing. 'I'm sorry. I've . . . killed your brother. I shot him.'" She looked up at Busher, who looked troubled and anxious. She looked at her hands, clasped in front of her. *Damn you!* "Do you want some coffee?" she asked. "Maybe some beer?"

Busher shook his head. "No. Just go on."

She nodded. "Of course. I asked him, '*When did you shoot my brother?*' And he said, 'A week ago.' I said, 'Where?'" She stopped again; the tears returned, and all at once she didn't want to continue because it was so very tiresome to talk while the memories were crowding back. It was

137

wearisome even to think. She got the idea that
this man wanted to spar with her, and it was
something she did not want to do.

"Something wrong, Miss Nichols?" he said.
She tried in vain to detect a genuine note of concern in his voice.

Damn you! "Nothing's wrong," she told him.
"This is just very difficult, so very difficult . . ."
Hang on tight, sis!

"Yes," Busher said, "I can understand that."

"And I think we should be out there"—she
gestured toward the back of the house, toward
the fields behind it—"looking for Jason's
body . . ." *Damn you, goddamn you! Hang on
tight, sis, hang on tight! That's right! Now
doesn't that feel good?*

"In time, Miss Nichols. In the morning, when
it's light and we're not tripping all over each
other. After all . . ." He stopped.

"After all," she went on for him, "Jason's dead,
so what does it matter? Is that what you were
going to say?"

He nodded. "It was," he answered.

She looked away. "The man said that he . . .
buried Jason." She heard a sharp and sudden in-
take of breath from Busher. "He didn't say
where, exactly," she went on, voice quivering.
"He said, 'Out behind your house, miss. Out

138

where the ground's fertile.' " She stopped. She felt a strange little smile crease her lips. She went on, "Those were his words, exactly. And so I asked him of course to tell me what he meant. I asked him why he was trying to turn the whole thing into a puzzle. I told him that he'd done enough, hadn't he? Killing Jason in the first place, accident or not." She became aware that she'd been slurring her words because she was trying to keep tears back. *Damn you!*

"You'll have to speak more clearly, Miss Nichols," the deputy said.

She nodded, smiled again, in apology this time. "I'm sorry, please understand—"

"I do understand."

"I hope so." She heard an odd, pleading quality in her voice, which puzzled her. "That's all he said, and then he hung up."

Chapter Twenty

1931

The fire that destroyed all of Orchid Street, except for the house Katherine Nichols would live in fifty-one years later, started in the apartment Matthew Ungen shared with his dog, Jack, an aged mongrel crippled by arthritis and even older, in dog age, than his master's seventy-eight years.

It was the night following the killing of Christina Marchetti and the killing of Galen—whose body had not yet been discovered in the little gardening shed where his mother had put him—and it was five hours after the killing of Gloria.

Her killer hadn't moved her body, so it still lay naked, on its belly, near the sitting room entrance, when Llewellyn Simms happened upon it forty-five minutes later. He came in the back

door. "I'm sorry, Gloria, forgive me," he said as
he moved through the kitchen, palette, brushes,
and oils under his arm. "But I've just been so
exhausted lately." He came out of the kitchen
and started down the well-lighted hallway. He
saw Gloria's body at once. He said her name, his
voice low and incredulous. He said it once, then
again, and again, as he moved slowly toward her.
He bent over, put a hand on her back. Her face
was turned to the right, eyes open. Her massive
arms were at her sides, palms up, and her legs
were straight, toes pointed toward the kitchen
behind her. "Gloria?" Llewellyn said. He knew
at once that she was dead, because breathing had
always been hard for her, so her body heaved
with the effort. It was very still now. And her
skin was cool. He thought that it probably felt
good to her. She had always despised the heat.

He managed to roll her over, though it took a
gargantuan effort. A long, rolling, burping sound
came from her, and he stood and looked sadly at
her. "Gloria," he said again. He grabbed hold of
her arms. Fifteen minutes later, he succeeded in
dragging her into the sitting room, to the base of
the delicate Queen Anne chair in which she had
always posed. "Gloria," he said once more. And
a half hour after that, with immense effort, he
had seated her in the chair, with her head thrown

back—there was no way to prop it up—and her hands clasped, her feet together. She had turned a dense shade of mottled blue and pink.

He would use a small canvas, he decided. And she would crowd it on all sides because she was a big woman in so many ways, so many wonderful ways. And he would frame it in dark wood, which was appropriate.

When the fire that destroyed most of Orchid Street started in Matthew Ungen's apartment, Llewellyn Simms was just putting the finishing touches on Gloria's death portrait. He thought it was very good, very honest, and very realistic.

Chapter Twenty-one

Katherine did not sleep. She served Deputy Sheriff Busher one cup of coffee after another, sat across from him in the living room, and watched almost without speaking as he drank.

"I'll be calling Whelan in the morning," he had told her. "In the meantime, I think it's probably best if I stay here with you."

"Uh-huh," she said.

"Because," he went on, in answer to a question she hadn't asked, "you never know, do you, what that . . . hunter is going to do?"

"Uh-huh," Katherine repeated.

"Something wrong?" he asked.

She shook her head. "I don't know," she whispered. "I'm . . . numb. I feel numb."

"I understand that," he said, smiling his reassurance. "But by tomorrow afternoon, believe me, it'll all be over."

She didn't answer that. She hoped he could see how unrealistic it was. "And then," he continued, "you can go back to doing . . . whatever it is that you do." He looked questioningly at her. "What *do* you do?"

She shook her head. "I paint. I have a degree in art." She sighed. "I paint a little. Thanks for asking."

He gave her a friendly smile. Katherine wasn't sure how she felt about him, about his round, pleasant, paternal face that could so easily move from one mood to another—from pleasantness to condemnation. "We'll wait," he said. "Feel free to go back to bed if you want."

"No," she said. *Putting on a show for the townies, sis?* "No," she repeated. "I'll wait with you. I don't think I could sleep."

At 6:00 the following morning, Busher called Whelan at his home in Jefferson, twenty-five miles away, and told him about Katherine's phone call. "She claims a man told her that he shot her brother the morning of his disappearance," Busher said. "She claims this man buried the body somewhere behind her house. He didn't say where, exactly. I'm at the house now and Miss Nichols is with me."

After a pause, Busher said, "Yes, sir. I'll be

sure of that." He hung up, looked at Katherine, standing nearby. "Whelan will be here inside the half hour. We'll start looking then."

Katherine nodded. "Yes," she whispered. "Good."

Whelan looked like a man who hadn't slept in days. He pushed into the house, followed again by a uniformed trooper, and the same plainclothes cop who had been with him before. "You remember Tom Dawson, Miss Nichols," he said, and she said hello, without enthusiasm; then Whelan went directly to Busher, complained brusquely about having to work on his day off, for which Busher gave him a quick apology, and Whelan came back to Katherine, took out a cigar, stuck it unlit into his mouth, and barked through clenched teeth, "Did you kill your brother, Miss Nichols?"

She'd expected the question. She looked him squarely in the eye—he smiled a little—and said crisply, "I've answered that question already, Mr. Whelan."

He said nothing. He chewed the unlit cigar, rolling it from one side of his mouth to the other, then turned to Busher. "Bring her," he said, then pushed his way from the house, the uniformed trooper and Dawson directly behind him.

Busher stepped forward and took hold of Katherine's arm. "Come on with me," he said, and gestured toward the door.

She said, "Am I under arrest?"

"Arrest?" He shook his head. "Of course you're not under arrest." A smile of reassurance and what Katherine guessed was pretended surprise appeared on his face. "Mr. Whelan needs you, that's all." Again he gestured toward the door.

Together they left the house.

Many of the same men who had been involved in the search that ended just a day earlier showed up that morning. They talked with excitement amongst themselves, gesturing obliquely now and again at Katherine, who was standing stiffly with Busher waiting for Whelan to question her. They got shovels out of the backs of their pickup trucks, and the trunks of their cars. A few pickaxes were hauled out, too, and one man brought a few dogs—a bloodhound, a German shepherd, and a collie—led them over to Katherine, and commanded, "Sniff, sniff!" until Whelan ran over and pushed the man away.

"Thanks," Katherine managed.

"For what?" Whelan said, clearly not expecting an answer, and went off again to talk to Dawson.

It was working into a very warm and uncomfortable morning. Katherine had dressed in jeans and a flannel shirt and she could feel a nervous perspiration starting. She said to Busher, "I don't understand the delay. Why doesn't he get started?"

"In his own good time," Busher said, and Katherine could tell from his tone that he didn't want to elaborate.

She said, nonetheless, "Why does he think I killed my brother?"

"I'm not sure he does."

"I am." *Hang on tight, sis!*

"He's just thinkin' about all the possibilities, that's all," Busher said.

"Perhaps," Katherine said. "But I resent it." *Now doesn't that feel good?*

Busher said, in a very paternal way, "Of course you do."

Whelan came over, stuck another unlit cigar into his mouth, and began chewing on it. "Tell me what this man who called you said, Miss Nichols." He took the cigar from his mouth, held it close to lips, continued, "I want his words verbatim, even the intonation, if possible."

She repeated what she had told Busher the previous evening.

When she was done, Whelan said, "Tell me again."

She reluctantly began to repeat it and Whelan cut in, "Intonation, Miss Nichols. I want to know *how* he said what he said. Do you understand?"

"Yes. I know what *intonation* means," she answered, and told him again what she'd told Busher the previous evening.

When she was done, Whelan said, "It doesn't really *mean* much, does it?" He gestured expansively at the fields behind the house. "Look here, it's *all* fertile, isn't it?"

Katherine said nothing; she assumed his question had been rhetorical.

"Well," he said, "isn't it?"

She nodded. "Sure, I guess it is."

He nodded quickly. "Damn right." He grinned at her. "But it's a nice speech, anyway, Miss Nichols." And before she could reply, he turned, marched over to where the townies and the several state troopers had gathered, and led them into the fields behind the house.

Busher followed; when he was a few yards away, he looked back: "We're going to need you, Miss Nichols," he said, and yet another of his fatherly smiles lit up his face.

"Why?" she said, and asked again, "Am I under arrest?"

He came slowly and thoughtfully back to where she was standing, at the bottom of her back porch steps, put his arm around her waist, coaxed her forward, toward the fields, and explained, his voice soft and apologetic, "No. You're not under arrest. We're going to need you to identify your brother's body, that's all."

By midmorning, a number of holes of varying depths had been dug in the twenty acres of field behind Katherine's house. One of the holes yielded the badly rusted iron barrel of an ancient flintlock, which Whelan thought was a wonderful discovery. Another hole yielded some planking for what could have been, he theorized, a box of some kind. But none of the holes yielded Jason's body, and so a break was called and a half dozen members of the search party, plus Whelan, Busher, the uniformed trooper, and Detective Dawson, filed into the house, after Katherine, then into the kitchen.

"Coffee!" someone hollered, and there was a general murmur of assent. Katherine set about making the coffee, aware as she did so that the mood was turning almost festive, and she found herself resenting the townies who'd shown up, because they had obviously shown up not to be helpful, but because there was a good chance that one of them would find Jason's body, and it would be something to crow about for years. There was probably even a betting pool, maybe several of them, one for *who* would find Jason's body, another for *where,* another for the type of wound, another for the position of the body, another for its depth . . .

Katherine had taken a large, white ceramic container of Starbucks coffee from the cupboard, and as she carried it from the cupboard to the counter, she dropped it, unable to hold on to it in her agitation. It clunked to the wood floor, but did not break. *Hang on tight, sis!* She grabbed the counter with both hands, lowered her head. "Damn you!" she whispered, started to say it again, glanced about. No one had seemed to notice. "Damn you, Jason!" *Hang on tight, sis!*

A minute passed, then another, until at last someone yelled, above the din of voices in the small room, "Hey, where the hell's the coffee at?"

Katherine cursed him, too, at a whisper, then bent over and picked up the jar of coffee.

"It's coming," she called, and heard the small, quivering note of apology in her voice.

* * *

At 11:15, when the break was declared over and the searchers had filed back outside, a ragged line of dense gray storm clouds had appeared at the eastern horizon and the air had become still and miserably hot. Several of the searchers, complaining all the while, abandoned the search. Katherine heard one of these men say loudly, "Jesus, *she* ain't gonna tell us where she put him!"

This left eight townies, three uniformed troopers, Detective Dawson, and Whelan, plus the dogs that one of the townies had brought along. Whelan nodded at the dogs. "Hey," he said to their owner, a thin, middle-aged, and ill-shaven man in blue overalls, "do you think they're doing any real good here?"

"Mebbe," the man answered. "They's a lotta smells in there, now"—he gestured toward the fields—"and these dogs is good, you know, but they ain't as good as genu-wine tracking dogs, which I ain't got the money for."

Whelan told him brusquely that they'd been using "genu-wine tracking dogs" all week, to no avail, and that maybe it was best if these dogs were parked somewhere.

"Sure," the man said, looking a little hurt, and took the dogs to his pickup truck, where he shooed them into the cab.

Chapter Twenty-two

1931

The fire that destroyed all but one house on Orchid Street started in Matthew Ungen's kitchen and spread quickly. It started because Matthew was trying to keep his dog warm, even though it was an August evening and the temperature would not drop to below eighty until after midnight. Matthew's dog suffered from arthritis, so the dry heat that the woodstove produced soothed him and eased his pain. "We'll go down to Arizona, Jack, one of these days," Matthew told the dog that evening. The fire started moments later.

It was a gasoline fire, very hot and very quick. Matthew had been storing gasoline in the kitchen in glass canning jars, all of which were tightly lidded, except one. He'd been storing gasoline because he was giving serious thought to converting his cooking stove to gasoline. No one had to tell him that gasoline was a dangerous substance to store in his kitchen; he wasn't a stupid man, but he was a man on a rapid downslide into senility, and so he was a little forgetful. He had been planning to move the gasoline to a safer place, but Jack, his dog, had a tiny spasm that evening that caused him to kick out and knock over several of the canning jars, including the one that was open. It spilled its contents, the fumes spread, and within moments, the kitchen exploded. Once, then again, and a third time, as the canning jars popped.

A stiff westerly wind that night pushed through Matthew's open windows and did a good job of fanning the flames in his kitchen and pushing them into the rest of the house, which ignited almost instantly because it was old, dry, and choked with old, dry collectibles.

But it was not the wind itself that pushed the fire down the rest of Orchid Street. A woman named Wilhelmina, who lived next door to Matthew, did that. She awoke from a short nap, saw the flames, and ran from her house to Matthew's house screaming, "Fire, fire!" And it was to her credit as a human being that she threw Matthew's side door open and stepped inside. Her concern, at that moment, was for him, and she could not have known that the inside of his house had become an inferno, that the very air was hot enough to ignite her clothes and her hair and turn her into a creature possessed of only one thought—to escape the awful flames that had become as much a part of her as her skin.

And so she ran back to her house—arms flying, and a ragged scream tearing from her throat—and ignited it. At that point, her thoughts were only of escaping the incredible, searing pain, so she ran from her house to the next house, ignited it, then started across the narrow street. She made it halfway before collapsing in a blackened heap. The second house she'd ignited did the work of carrying the flames across the street. White cotton long johns, a bright green taffeta dress, and a homemade bedspread hung out to dry on the house's front porch were lifted, flaming gaily, into the summer night by a stiff wind and thrown across the street.

The city fire department, such as it was, had been notified of the developing conflagration at 8:10, far too late for an adequate response. By the time the first trucks arrived, half the street was ablaze and the strong wind was pushing the flames from one house to the next in rapid succession.

Two of the three hydrants on the street had rusted shut long ago, and both—because of a deteriorating water supply system—had inadequate pressure anyway. The third hydrant had pressure, but it was at the east end of the street, where the fire had begun, and where there was only one structure left to save, number 8, a sturdy, cream-colored, wood-frame house not unlike most of the other houses on the street. It was the house that Katherine Nichols would move into fifty-one years later.

At 2:00 A.M., most of the fires had burned themselves out, and a few houses, at the west end of the street, were still standing, but were gutted. They would be destroyed by bulldozers within a week.

And within a year, number 8 Orchid Street would be moved, for sentimental reasons, to its beautiful and idyllic country setting near Honeoye, the rest of the street's houses bulldozed into their basements and a five-year effort begun to turn the entire area into a city park. No one involved in the project realized the multitude of sins that the bulldozers were covering up.

Chapter Twenty-three

Jason's body was found at a little past noon, just before the storm, which had been threatening for much of the morning, broke at last. The body had been buried in the small gardening plot fifty feet behind Katherine's house. The grave had been well concealed; large, weed-clotted chunks of earth had apparently been removed, vegetation intact; a three-by-seven-by-three-foot trench had then been dug in the subsoil, and Jason laid into it. The intact square chunks of earth and weeds had then been laid over him, like turf. The grave might have gone undiscovered for a long while were it not for the fact that in removing the squares of earth, the killer had destroyed a good number of the weed and grass root systems— enough, in fact, that eight days later, a rough but unmistakable outline of the burial trench was visible when viewed from just the right angle.

It was the man with the dogs who discovered the trench. His name was O'Hanlon, and he made the discovery just as he was coming out of the kitchen's back door, and the garden area was below him and to his left, so his perspective was good. A quivering smile of disbelief spread over O'Hanlon's thin face. He called to anyone who might be listening—and at that point, most of the searchers were well into the fields, except for Detective Dawson, who was close to the garden area—"Hey, I think I found the sucker!" And he ran stiffly into the garden and began tearing up the clods of weeds and earth with his bare hands.

He uncovered Jason immediately. First his stomach, then his chest. O'Hanlon stopped there, quivering with excitement. He felt someone beside him; he reached. "Leave it be!" Dawson commanded. "This is a crime scene, now." And he grabbed O'Hanlon's arm.

"I just wanna see his face is all!" O'Hanlon pleaded.

Dawson grimaced. "Don't let it worry you. We'll all get a chance to see his face."

Reluctantly, O'Hanlon backed off, and Dawson heard from behind him, "Mr. Dawson, have you found him?" He turned. Katherine was on her back porch, arms stiff at her sides, fists clenched. From her tone, Dawson thought, she could have been asking if he'd found a set of missing car keys. He saw also that what could have been a smile was playing on her lips. He had seen such smiles before on the faces of survivors. They were nervous smiles, smiles of relief that a particular nightmare was over. Tears often accompanied such smiles.

Dawson stood and nodded grimly. "Yes, Miss Nichols, I believe we've found your brother."

The other searchers started trickling over. Two of the uniformed troopers, first, then several of the townies, then Whelan, who ran a half mile from an area near the stand of woods. He pushed through the circle of men, his breathing irregular and heavy, and stood next to Jason's body for several moments. Then he bent over and pulled off the clod of earth and weeds that had been covering Jason's shoulders and head.

Someone in the crowd whispered, "Holy shit! Look at that!"

Jason had been shot in the face, and consequently much of it was missing. Insects and larvae were rolling and tumbling and munching on what remained.

Someone toward the rear of the group retched, and someone else said, "Hey, c'mon, you got it on my fuckin' shoe!"

Katherine stepped off the porch and came

slowly forward. Whelan saw her out of the corner of his eye and raised his hand, palm out: "No, Miss Nichols!" he commanded, then turned his head to look at her. "No!" he repeated, but she quickened her pace. Whelan cursed, pushed back through the circle of men, and ran over to her. He was still breathing hard. "No!" he said again, and put his hands hard around her arms.

"I need to identify him," Katherine said, voice quivering.

Whelan said, "Miss Nichols, there's nothing to *identify!*"

She looked him squarely in the eye. He could see that her mouth was breaking into a thankful, desperate grin. She whispered, "Yes, I understand that," then broke free, maneuvered around him like a nimble linebacker, and ran to where Jason lay. She was silent for a few moments. Then she screamed.

Whelan, who had turned and run after her at once, grabbed her from behind, around the shoulders, and pulled her away. She continued screaming. Some of the townies, looking on, had their mouths open. One of them said to a friend, "Good act, huh?" His friend nodded in agreement.

Katherine continued screaming until, in her kitchen, the scream broke into a sob, at last, and she looked up, from where she had seated herself at her little kitchen table, and said to Whelan, standing over her, "It was so ugly! It was so *ugly!* Jason wasn't ugly!" To which Whelan said nothing at all.

It was nearly four hours before the last of the searchers left, including Whelan, who nodded at the county pathologist's station wagon, hauling Jason's body away, and said, "He'll get the answers for us, Miss Nichols. You can count on it."

Katherine watched him drive off from behind her closed front door. When his car had disappeared over the little rise a couple of hundred yards west of the house, she whispered after him, "Damn you, goddamn you!" and felt better for it, because she had never hated anyone quite so much as she hated him. She turned and went into the kitchen. She couldn't bring herself to prepare a meal, but she was hungry nonetheless. She opened a cupboard, withdrew a loaf of rye bread, took a slice out, and began munching at it. It tasted good. It stimulated her appetite. She pushed it into her mouth, felt her saliva working on it, enjoyed the feel of it. *Hang on tight, sis!* She worked it into mush, swallowed, took another slice, pushed it into her mouth, chewed

163

hungrily, swallowed, took another. *Now doesn't that feel better!*

She thought then that she'd like something on it. Something light. Some mayonnaise, maybe some peanut butter. She checked her cupboards. No peanut butter. She took the loaf of bread to the refrigerator, peered in. She found that she had no mayonnaise, either. She had tahini spread, which possessed an inoffensive, vaguely nutty taste. She took the jar of tahini spread to the counter, got a butter knife from a drawer beneath. *Hang on tight, sis. Right around there. That's good.* She spread a slice of the bread thickly with the tahini spread. She studied the results in silence and thought at last that she'd like to put a top on it, make it into a sandwich. *Now doesn't that feel good? Damn you!* She put a top on it, studied it again, took the top off, went back to the refrigerator with it, opened the meat drawer. *Damn you, goddamn you!* There was some sliced turkey. It was several days old and turning dark red around the edges. She took it out, carried it to the counter, cut the reddish areas away, and layered it with the tahini spread. She put the top back on the sandwich, sniffed it. *Damn you, goddamn you!* She ate the sandwich very slowly, savoring each bite. Nothing had ever tasted so good.

When she was done with it, the phone rang. She answered it at once, annoyed at the interruption.

"Yes?" she said.

"Hello, Katherine," she heard. *Hang on tight, sis.* It was Larry Cage.

From just beyond a half dozen windows in the house, in the muggy, late afternoon aftermath of the storm, under a deep blue August sky, things that had once been eyes, in things that had once been faces, watched her in silence. She did not see them, although, as she talked to her erstwhile lover, she turned her body now and again, and her gaze passed from window to window and held at each one momentarily. She saw her land (her fields, her garden, her stand of poplars), and she got a nice, comfortable sense of belonging that she had never felt before, not even as a child on her family's Vermont estate. And she saw also what she supposed were tiny waves of heat rising up.

"Jason is dead," she told Larry Cage, a few clumsy pleasantries already disposed of.

A short silence on the other end of the line, then: "Jason? Your brother?"

Katherine smiled a little at the question. "Someone shot him." *A hunter. Some ignorant*

165

bastard with a narrow face and close-set, vacant eyes . . . "A hunter shot him."

"Christ, when did all this happen?"

"Last week. A week ago," she answered. "That's when he was shot, anyway. Last week. It was an accident." The image of what had been left of her brother's face came screaming back to her—*Zombies, sis! No, you gotta stand still!*—and she hurried on, her voice rising in pitch and volume, as if the noise would push the awful image away, "It was an accident, as I said, and when this hunter shot him, after he shot him, he buried him out behind the house, in the garden, to cover it up."

"In the garden?"

"Yes, to cover it up," she repeated. "And then his conscience got the better of him, I guess his conscience got the better of him, because he called me and told me what he'd done."

"Good God—"

"That was just last night, in fact." The image of what remained of Jason's face began to recede. Her voice slowed and quieted. "About six or six-thirty. He called. He told me what he'd done. He was sorry for it. He was very apologetic. He said that accidents happened all the time." *Now doesn't that feel good, sis? Didn't I tell you that would feel good?* "He told me . . . he made a lit-

166

tle puzzle out of finding Jason's body. He told me, 'Where the ground is fertile.' *My, but aren't you beginning to bud nicely?* " 'Where the ground is fertile,' " she repeated. "It was a little puzzle. He was trying to make it hard for us, I think. But we found Jason. We found him. In the garden." She realized that she was repeating herself. She took a breath. "Do I sound upset, Larry?"

"Of course you do."

"I am." She paused. Her stomach was churning. "Larry?"

"Yes?"

"I've got to leave the phone for just a moment, just . . ." She put her hand to her stomach. ". . . a moment." She let the receiver drop. *Hang on tight, sis!* She closed her eyes against the wave of nausea that washed over her. *Hang on tight!* "Damn you!" she whispered. "Damn you!" *Now doesn't that feel better?* The nausea passed. She picked up the receiver. "Tahini spread and rotten turkey, Larry," she said. "I should have known better."

Silence.

"Larry?"

"Are you alone, Katherine?"

"Yes, I am."

"I'm coming out there. Right now."

"Larry, that's not necessary."

"I want to. I want to very much. I'll see you in an hour. I love you." He hung up.

Katherine hung up.

Her gaze settled on the living room windows, on the line of poplars beyond, on the ripples of heat rising in the August air.

Chapter Twenty-four

Oddly, she could not remember what Larry looked like, exactly. She remembered that his eyes were gray, his hair dark brown, that he was nicely muscled and carried himself well. But she could not form an exact mental image of him. She knew why. She had pushed him away. She had erased him from her memory because that memory was painful. He was a bully. He wanted to push her around and tell her how to live. And all because she had made a few bad choices, all because she was malleable.

He was coming back. She didn't want him back—she knew that as strongly as she knew anything. She wanted solitude. She wanted to breathe for herself, at last, and *do* for herself, and not be suffocated by him, and sheltered by him, as he always had, as so many others in her life had—Jason, her father, the religious cult.

But Larry was coming back, anyway. Even though he knew she didn't really want him back. That fact made no difference within the kind of greedy love he had for her.

She tried to eat again, while she waited for him to arrive, but she did not enjoy it as she had enjoyed it earlier, so she gave it up and left her plate almost full—lettuce, tomato slices, a scoop of tuna salad. A very civilized meal, unlike the one she had eaten earlier.

She sat on her living room floor, lights off, and watched the darkness come. She remembered doing the same thing only a month and a half earlier, just before buying the house. She remembered liking the way the house felt around her, and thinking that she was going to be happy in it. She wasn't certain of that anymore. Not with Larry coming back.

She slipped her arms around her knees, clasped her hands, and bent forward. *Hang on tight, sis!* She wondered if she could hide in the darkness in this house. From Larry. From Whelan and his accusations. And she wondered how alike the two men were, and if they wanted basically the same thing from her—her freedom. *Zombies, sis. You gotta stay still!* But then, she thought, Larry didn't smoke cigars, and he wasn't overweight. She smiled.

The phone rang. She turned her head sharply toward the sound; it was coarse, she thought, and impolite, and she didn't want to answer it. But she did answer it, thinking it was Larry. It wasn't. It was Whelan.

"We've got the autopsy report, Miss Nichols," he said. "I thought you'd be interested."

"Yes?" she said.

"It says that your brother was killed with a hunting rifle. A thirty-thirty. At close range."

"Close range? How close?"

"Within ten feet." Whelan said. "Do you own a thirty-thirty, Miss Nichols?"

"Why would I own a rifle, Mr. Whelan? I don't hunt. I've never hunted!" She felt a twinge of nausea come up, then retreat.

"So you don't own one?"

"I wouldn't have one in the house, Mr. Whelan."

"Uh-huh." A short pause. "He was dragged from where he was shot. Quite a distance, too. There were several different kinds of dirt layered into the backs of his shoes."

"Of course he was dragged, Mr. Whelan."

"Sorry? I don't understand."

"If he'd been shot near the house," she explained, "I would have heard."

"And you heard nothing?"

"That's correct."

"Of course it is." Another pause. Then, "Keep yourself available to us, please."

"I will," she said, hung up, and burst into tears.

Larry Cage took the turn onto Garnsey Road from the Old Post Road. He slowed the car; the road was worn and it was dusk, a bad time for seeing.

He'd been practicing a speech all the way down from the city. He'd said it a number of times, to himself, as he drove, changing it a little each time, to achieve the greatest impact. It went like this:

"First of all, and most importantly, I love you, Katherine. And I don't think there's anything, *anything,* more important than that fact. The fact that I love you, and you love me. The fact that we're *in love.*" A pause. A slight smile. "Do you know how very wonderful and unique that is in this world, Katherine? And what a responsibility it puts on us, as people?" Another pause; the smile dissipates and is replaced by a look of deep concern. "We are an *example,* because we are in love." Let it sink in. It was important. *Love* was important to her—it didn't matter very much where it came from. "Because we have the sort of magnanimous, selfless love that is so good for the world." Which might remind her a little of the cult she'd been a part of, so maybe he'd have to rephrase that part of the speech. "So good for the world," he'd continue. "And for us." Another pause, then the kicker: "And for our children, because *that's* where it's really at, Katherine!"

He thought it was a pretty good speech. For his own tastes, it was a little heavy on the *What can we do for our fellow man?* stuff, but he could live with it. The speech had punch and simplicity, and it had that great kicker. Doubtless, it would work.

Of course, it was very important to steer clear of mentioning Jason. Because he was the monkey wrench, the fly in the ointment. She'd get all glassy-eyed and mumbly talking about him. Poor, sick bastard! And if he did come up during on their conversations, he'd simply tell her that she had to put the whole affair behind her; that she had her memories of him, and after all, what else did anyone have in life but memories? In time she'd come to realize that she was much better off without him hanging around, trying to get at her.

He turned his headlights on. He was nearing the house. He thought he could see it at the front of the line of poplars, which were silhouetted against the dark blue, eastern sky, and swaying gracefully in a slight breeze.

He saw, as he drove closer to the house, that Katherine had apparently not turned the lights on, yet. Just like the last time he was here, he remembered. And since he was a reluctant believer in omens, he thought that this was not a good one.

He slowed the car (a way of putting off what he knew was going to be an uncomfortable situation, regardless of his punchy speech). And when he was within fifty yards of the house and his headlights were on the living room windows, he stopped, because he was seeing something there, in the glare of the headlights, that he didn't understand. Something that frightened him.

He was seeing people at the side of the house. Five people standing at the living room windows and looking in—a tall man and a naked woman who was very fat, a thin, scruffy-looking boy with no shoes, a dark-haired woman with an aura of great sadness about her, and a small, dark-haired child. And they were not reacting to the headlights, except to look back now and then, stoically, as if they were looking through the headlights, at Larry himself. And they were talking among themselves with great excitement, Larry thought, because their heads were nodding

174

and their arms were moving rapidly about.

And as Larry watched them, as he was about to get out of the car and approach them to ask who they were and what in the hell they thought they were doing, they moved away from the light—two to the north, two to the south, and the thin, scruffy boy in Larry's direction, toward the light, as if he were drawn to it. And watching him, Larry could see, at last, what it was that was so frightening and so confusing about these people, and about this boy. They were approximations. Half-formed. Half-finished. Like oil paintings in progress. They had no eyes, only the suggestion of eyes, and no arms, or hands or legs, only the suggestion of arms and hands and legs. As if something real and tangible were moving behind a fogged window.

It was the way that Larry saw the thin, scruffy boy moving slowly toward him in the glare of the headlights. As if the windshield were fogged, although the house, in the light, was clear, and the poplars, and the hood of the car, and the road.

Larry lowered his head, covered his eyes with his fists, and screamed.

Then he let his hands fall and looked up, into the August night, into what the glare of the headlights showed him—the house, the front edges of the poplars, moving slightly in a gentle breeze, the road. He asked himself what more he could have seen than that. He asked it in desperation, as if trying to recall the sanity that was trying hard to leave him. He succeeded. He was an intelligent man and strong-willed, and he could make order out of disorder when it was necessary, as it was at that moment.

He heard, next to his open window, "My God, Larry, why were you screaming?"

He turned his head sharply, saw Katherine bending over to look through the car window.

"Hello," he said, and made a feeble attempt at a smile.

She asked again, "Why were you screaming, Larry?"

He looked away, at the house again. "I was, wasn't I? I remember that I was. But I don't know why. I can't remember why." It was the truth. "I saw something that frightened me."

"What was it?"

He shook his head. "I don't know. I can't remember. Nothing, obviously, otherwise I'd remember." He grinned a little.

Katherine opened the door. "Come inside, Larry. We'll talk."

An image returned to him from just a minute before—strange people clustered at Katherine's window, a strange boy moving toward the car.

He flinched, pushed the image away, got out of the car. "Did I scare you, Katherine?" He gave her a quick, self-conscious kiss. "I'm sorry if I did."

She closed the car door gently. "It's okay," she told him. "You didn't scare me—I think I'm beyond being scared." And they went into the house.

Chapter Twenty-five

They made love violently, each giving the other a lot of pain. It was a new kind of lovemaking for them both, and when it was done they rolled to their backs and breathed heavily, saying nothing, for far longer than they needed because it was a way of postponing talking about their lovemaking, a way of putting it behind them.

Katherine was first to break the silence. "I miss Jason," she said, and during the brief pause that followed, Larry could hear his speech, which he'd practiced all the way down in the car, coming back to him, running around in his brain, begging to be said. Then he felt Katherine's hand take his in the darkness, and she added, "I'm sorry. That was a foolish thing to say."

"I understand," he said.

"Do you?"

"Yes." He paused; perhaps, he thought, he understood it too well. The thought made him cringe. He hurried on, "It's been very bad for you, I know."

"Yes, it has."

"That was a dumb remark. I'm sorry." He gave a moment to silence. "Can we talk?"

"Yes."

He glanced at her, puzzled by her terse replies and her matter-of-fact attitude. "About us?"

"We can talk about anything you'd like, Larry."

"I was just thinking about . . . what we have together . . . the two of us—"

"I don't want any of your speeches, Larry."

He stiffened. "Any of my speeches?" He tried to sound offended.

"They're very good, honestly. Very convincing and persuasive. Sometimes I even enjoy them. But I don't want to hear one right now."

He rolled his head away from her and let go of her hand. Words would not come to him.

"Does that offend you?" she asked. He noted the vaguest touch of concern in her voice.

"Of course it does, Katherine."

"I don't want it to offend you. I just want us to be truthful with each other from now on."

"From now on?"

"You want to come back to me, don't you?"

180

He looked at her, caught her gaze, and mumbled something incoherent. Happiness was welling up inside him and making him feel clumsy.

"Don't you?" she coaxed.

"You're not even going to . . ." His smile broadened and he wondered if he looked like a fool. "You're not even going to let me use my speech on you? I mean, I practiced it all the way here, and it really is one of my best."

"No. Please, no!" It was a tight, harsh whisper.

He pushed on, anyway, unwilling to admit her quick change of mood. "Not even a little tiny bit, the teeniest, tiniest bit . . ." He stopped. He saw that her fists were clenched and her lips tight. "Okay," he said. "No speeches."

She said nothing.

"Really, Katherine, I'm sorry."

"Don't be sorry, Larry. And please, please—don't smother me. You always smother me."

"I wasn't aware . . ."

"Of course you weren't. Why would you be? It's your nature."

"I'll change my nature, Katherine."

"You'll have to."

"I will, believe me, I will."

"For both our sakes, Larry, I hope that you do."

181

Part Two
Friends

Chapter Twenty-six

They settled nicely into their house and their new situation. Katherine put off starting a garden until the following year because, she explained, it was much too late to begin one that year. "You have to plant early in the spring, Larry," she said, and he wondered if she ever would start one—in the garden area, anyway. Where Jason had been put. He decided that if she did, she was a lot stronger than he thought.

She got back into her painting, instead, which she'd neglected in her first several weeks at the house. She set her easel up in many places—in the house itself (where she did quick studies of its six rooms from various angles)—on the back porch, in the fields behind the house. She painted well, but now, Larry thought, with a new kind of pinched and obsessive realism that too often gave her finished work a static look.

Jason was not mentioned often. Once, before an outing, Larry had suggested, with what he thought was marvelous magnanimity, that they go visit Jason's graveside, in a little country cemetery a half hour's drive away.

"Wouldn't you like that, Katherine?" he said, and smiled a big, self-congratulatory smile.

They were on their way to the car. She was walking ahead of him, picnic basket in hand. She stopped. Stiffened.

"Katherine?" Larry said, a little unnerved, because he could see her face reflected in the driver's window and though he saw it unclearly, he detected immense tension in it. But when she turned toward him, he saw that she was smiling a thank-you.

"I don't think so, Larry," she said. "Maybe some other time. I think it would be hard to find the grave, anyway. The stone's not up, yet. I guess they wait for the ground to settle for that."

"Yes, they do."

"And besides, maybe it's a bit too soon . . ."

"I can understand that."

"I mean, I still dream about it—about finding him there—"

"I thought someone else found him. One of the townies."

186

"Yes. That's true. It was a man named O'Hanlon. But I was watching and I knew . . ." Which was where she let the subject drop.

At the beginning of their second week at the house, after Katherine had settled into familiar and comfortable routines—Larry commuted daily, a ninety-mile round trip that he gladly suffered, for her sake; she stayed at the house and painted, or took an occasional drive into Honeoye—that Kennedy Whelan called again.

Katherine recognized his voice at once. "What do you want, Mr. Whelan?"

"Just a little talk, Miss Nichols."

She took a quick, agitated breath, said, "About my brother? His case is closed. You said his case was closed."

"That's something we like to say." She imagined that he smiled. "In this instance, it's not really true, of course."

"And if I don't want to talk?"

"Then we won't. Very simple."

"Is it?"

"Simple? Not actually. You're an intelligent woman, Miss Nichols—"

"Just get on with it, Mr. Whelan."

"Of course." A brief pause. "I asked you about the gun, didn't I?"

187

"Yes, you did."

"And you told me what?"

"That I didn't have one." She heard what sounded like pages being flipped; then:

"No, actually, that's not what you said. You said, and I quote, 'I wouldn't have one in the house,' meaning the rifle, of course. And before that"—again the sound of pages being flipped—"you said, quoting once more, 'Why would I own a rifle, Mr. Whelan? I don't hunt. I've never hunted.' Do you remember saying that?"

She took another quick, agitated breath. Didn't he understand? Sometimes a person had to put things behind her, cut herself off. It was essential. And sometimes it was easy. "Yes," she said. "I remember saying that."

"And it's the truth?"

"Yes, it's the truth."

"And you don't recall, Miss Nichols, that as a child on your family's estate in Vermont you did quite a lot of hunting, and that you were, in fact, pretty good at it?"

Damn you, goddamn you! "Of course I recall that." *Hang on tight, sis!*

"Then perhaps you'd like to change your testimony?"

"It wasn't *testimony,* for Christ's sake! It was

a remark made under stress. Yes, of course I remember hunting. I remember that I enjoyed it. I remember I was very good at it. I remember it. But I was someone else, Mr. Whelan. I was a child and there were . . . influences on me that were very toxic." She stopped. She realized that she was beginning to sound strange. She went on, more slowly, "I was a *child,* Mr. Whelan. A child who very naturally enjoyed doing something she was good at. Especially if it pleased her father. But I grew out of that. I grew away from it. I am someone else, now. I haven't hunted in almost twenty years."

"No?"

"No!"

"You didn't go hunting for your brother, Miss Nichols? You didn't go hunting for him because you were having an incestuous relationship with him, and you—"

She hung up. *Damn you, goddamn you! Hang on tight, sis!* She called him back. As soon as he answered, she told him, "I will say this only once, Mr. Whelan. Even if you get me on some damned witness stand, I will not say it again. I did *not* kill my brother. I had no reason to kill him. I was *not* having an incestuous relationship with him, and I do not—I will repeat this—I do *not* own a

189

gun of any kind. I haven't owned a gun in a long,
long time. I do not *intend* to own a gun. If you
want my brother's killer, it is the man who called
me. The hunter. Now, beyond what I have just
said, Mr. Whelan, no more words will pass between us." She hung up and stood quietly with
her head bowed, eyes closed, arms stiff, and her
hand clutching the receiver. She thought, *Now
doesn't that feel better!*

The telephone rang while she was clutching it.
She snatched the receiver up and hissed into it,
"Damn you, goddamn you, I did *not* kill my
brother!" And she slammed the receiver down,
stepped back, and waited a full half hour, with
her eyes on the phone all the while. It did not
ring again.

Late that evening, after lovemaking

"It sounds like rain, Larry."

"Sorry?"

"I said it sounds like rain. Do you hear it?"

"There's no rain."

"I know that. I'm just telling you what I hear."

"I'm sorry, but I don't hear it." He glanced
toward the window. "Maybe a little."

"You hear it?"

He looked back at her. "Just a little. It could
be anything. It could be mice."

"I don't think it's mice. I've heard it before. I heard it yesterday."

"Oh?"

"Yes. And I think I saw it, too."

"That's an odd thing to say, Katherine. That you *think* you saw rain."

She smiled. "It made me feel good."

"Oh? You weren't feeling good?"

She shook her head. "Not really. Not fantastic. I was thinking about Jason, and about Mr. Whelan. And you, too."

He said nothing; he seemed to be waiting for her to elaborate.

She went on, "I was thinking that I've never been in much control of my life. I was thinking that I feel . . ." She faltered; she didn't know if she really wanted to continue.

Larry offered, "That you feel bullied?"

"Bullied? I don't know." She thought a moment. "Yes," she said. "Maybe."

"By me?"

"By you? Yes, I think so."

He sighed. "I'm sorry."

"I appreciate that, Larry, but it's not something I feel all the time. I don't feel it very often, in fact. Just every once in a while. Like yesterday. When I saw the rain and it made me feel good. Peaceful. Sometimes I need that very badly—to

191

feel peaceful. To have peace. And quiet."

"It could be mice, Katherine."

"The rain. You mean the sound of the rain?"

"Yes. Or termites."

"I had the house checked for termites, Larry. There aren't any. I could get a cat."

"No. I don't like cats. I don't like the way they skulk about. They're always skulking about."

She chuckled softly. "Spoken like a real male. But it's true. They skulk about. I like them, though. This house needs an animal. A cat would be nice."

"I said no, Katherine."

"I heard you, Larry." She thought of arguing with him, decided against it. It wasn't important. "I heard what you said," she repeated. There were things that were so much more important.

He said, "It's a little louder, now."

She listened. "Yes, I hear it. I think it's probably just the quack grass—"

"Quack grass?"

"Yes. Around the house. It's called quack grass. Didn't you know that?"

"No. Why would I?"

She shrugged. "I don't know. No reason." She looked away from him. "You're hard to get along with sometimes, Larry. Does lovemaking make you surly?"

"I didn't know I was being surly. I apologize."
She thought he didn't sound apologetic. He repeated, "I apologize. It was nice, by the way. Very nice."

"It usually is."

"Thanks."

"And I think I'm going to get a cat."

"I wish you wouldn't. I really wish you wouldn't. Besides, you're right—it's just the quack grass. Just the wind in the quack grass."

"That's very poetic, Larry. 'The wind in the quack grass.' Sort of like *The Wind in the Willows*. It stopped."

"Yes. I hear."

"It sounded like a bunch of people whispering to each other, don't you think?"

He made a noncommittal noise.

"A bunch of people whispering to each other in the quack grass," she went on, and smiled. "I think I'll paint that."

"Don't get a cat, Katherine."

"Okay, Larry. Okay."

"They're always skulking about."

"Christ," she said, "we all are."

"Is this working into an argument? If it is, I'd rather skip it."

She said nothing.

"Katherine?"

"I like that image. A bunch of people whispering to each other in the quack grass. Don't you like that image?"

"Sure. It's very poetic."

"You have no soul." She smiled. It was true, she thought. Larry really had no soul.

He said, "Just please, don't get a cat. Promise me."

"I promise."

"Thanks."

She rolled over, away from him. "Good night, Larry."

"Good night," he whispered.

Chapter Twenty-seven

Bill Straub had been hoping for weeks that Katherine was watching him every morning. He thought he looked pretty good now—lean and powerful, maybe even sexy.

"Sure she's older than me. I guess she's ten years older than me. Six or seven years, anyway," he told his best friend, Matthew, who was O'Hanlon's son. "But what the hell does that matter, huh?"

Matthew said, "I don't know. I ain't seen her, so I don't know. What's she, pretty hot?"

"Of course she's hot. Not that it matters."

"You mean, that if she looked a pile of cow shit you'd be fallin' all over yourself?"

"I ain't fallin' all over myself. Christ, Matthew!"

But he was and he hoped no one else had noticed. Especially Katherine.

He thought that he sure did run nice, though. And all women liked to watch a guy running. Especially a guy who was lean and powerful and maybe even sexy.

They liked to watch a guy's buns. And the bulge in his pants (it's what his sister said she liked to watch, anyway). And the way guys breathed, as if they were actually *doing it* while they were running.

He approached Katherine's house from the fields to the north, across the road. It was not quite 8:00 in the morning and the sun was casting long, dull shadows. He'd grown accustomed to seeing Katherine somewhere outside the house at this hour, with her easel set up. She nodded occasionally at him. And she smiled sometimes, too. And once, he remembered fondly, she had nodded and smiled and said, "Hi, Bill. Lookin' good!" At least, that was the way it had sounded at the time, from fifty yards away, beneath his labored breathing. But for sure there had been a look of appreciation on her face, anyway, as if she really had been enjoying whatever it was she'd been looking at (what his sister said that women looked at, maybe).

He saw her. She was near the line of poplars, her easel set up in front of her and her back to him. He slowed. She was dressed in blue shorts that fit snugly, and a white T-shirt. From his vantage point, just across the road, and about thirty yards away, he imagined that she was wearing no bra, and that as he passed her he'd have a hard time keeping his eyes off her, that if he wasn't careful he'd smack into one of the poplars and break his damned neck.

He saw a man standing to Katherine's left, about fifty feet from her, in tall grass close to the edge of the house, and he stopped running. Maybe, he thought at once, he should make a wide detour around the house. Maybe the man *knew* what was on his mind (because, Christ, every time he ran through here he got a damned hard-on that always took a *long* time to go away, and he was getting one now). And then he saw that the man, dressed in a dark blue suit, wasn't looking at him. He was looking at Katherine, and he was standing very still, as if he had been in the midst of movement—turning the corner of the house, maybe—then had stopping moving, because Katherine had taken him by surprise. Because maybe he was a burglar or a rapist. Bill retreated quickly from these ideas because they called for action, and he wasn't sure if he was up to it. Hell, the man was pretty big, bigger than he was, anyway, and chances were he was just a relative or something. Another brother, maybe, or maybe her father, which was more likely because he looked a lot older than she did. Or maybe he was a freakin' salesman, although there was no other car but hers in the driveway, and burglars and rapists probably didn't dress like this guy, in dark blue suits.

The man stepped back so he was hidden by the corner of the house.

Bill sprang forward, across the road. "Miss Nichols," he called urgently as he ran. She didn't turn to look. "Miss Nichols?" She cocked her head a little toward him. "Miss Nichols!" He was very close. She turned her head and looked questioningly at him. "Hello," she said quietly. He didn't hear her. "Miss Nichols!" He pointed wildly, stopped within arm's reach of her. She turned her body around to face him. "Hello," she said again, and a small, pleasant smile appeared on her face.

"Miss Nichols, there's someone—" He pointed again toward the side of the house, where the man had been. "There's someone watching you."

"No," she said, still smiling. "I don't think so."

"Yes, there was. And he was standing over there." He pointed toward the house.

"No," she repeated. Her smile vanished. "I don't think so. What's your name again?"

"Bill."

"I don't think anyone was watching me, Bill. But thank you for your concern."

"But, Miss Nichols—"

"Please, it's Katherine. You're early, aren't you?"

He glanced at the house, at the spot where the man had been, then at Katherine's chest, first, where his gaze lingered for several seconds, until he realized what he was doing, and then very self-consciously, he looked at her face. He saw that she was still smiling. "Early?" he said. "Maybe a few minutes." He became aware of the implications of her remark—that she had been taking notice of him every morning, and even of the time that he ran by. Pleasure started building inside him; then he started getting an erection, again. He felt himself blush violently, and turned sideways to her. "Maybe a few minutes," he repeated. Then he dashed off, down the path that Katherine had given him permission to use, toward the trees a half mile behind the house.

That evening

"What's this?" Larry asked.

Katherine looked. He was nodding at the painting she'd hung earlier in the day near the front door. He grinned and continued, "It's hideous, isn't it?"

"I don't think so," Katherine said. "I wouldn't have put it up if I thought so."

He considered a moment, then said, "I suppose." A brief pause. "Who is she?"

"I don't know. I found her upstairs, in a closet, when I moved in. I think the artist used to live in this house, and the woman in the painting is someone who lived on the street, I guess."

"The street?"

"Orchid Street. This house was brought here from Orchid Street, in the city. I told you that."

"Yes, I remember. I just don't remember that you told me the name of the street."

"I didn't." A brief pause, then, "It was quite a nice little street, apparently. Very comfortable and friendly. And she"—a nod at the painting—"lived on it. I like her."

"You like her?" He was incredulous.

"Yes. She looks friendly. She looks like someone I'd like to know."

"She looks *fat*, for Christ's sake!"

Katherine said nothing.

"She really is hideous," Larry said. "You've got to admit that. I mean, she might look friendly to you, but to me she's hideous, and if I've got to look at her every time I come in the door—"

"I'm not taking her down, Larry." There was

a tinge of anger in Katherine's voice. "I told you, I like her."

"She isn't even the right *color*, Katherine. She's kind of, I don't know . . ." He studied the painting closely for a moment. "She's kind of *blue!*"

"I know that. I can see that. It's an old painting. Oils change color over time. Under the right conditions."

He straightened. "Uh-huh. Whatever you say. But you don't mind if I look the other way when I come home, do you?"

"No, I don't mind," she answered. "You can do whatever you like."

Chapter Twenty-eight

Katherine could sense the dawn even through several layers of sleep and through several layers of clouds, and she had grown used to waking, then, an hour after Larry left the house. He left very early, to accommodate the long drive, and rising not too much later than he did gave her a good start on the day, as well as a chance to catch the morning light for her canvas.

This Friday morning, however, the end of their third week together at the house, she woke an hour late into a strange, soft darkness, as if there were heavy curtains between her and the morning sun. But the curtains over the room's one window had been left open.

She sat up in bed, uncertain of what she was seeing out that window. On some mornings, she saw low gray clouds tinged with red, and she thought that it was what she might be seeing, now, and that grogginess from too much sleep had altered the scene in some subtle way.

She threw the blanket off, got out of bed, took a few steps toward the window, looked.

Good Christ, she thought, *tell me I'm not seeing what I'm seeing!*

She was seeing a brick wall twenty feet beyond the window. The bricks were dirty, dark red, and chipped, as if from decades of wind and weather. In one corner of the wall, she could see the suggestion of a window.

And on her own window, she could see a fine layer of dust, as if a black mist had settled over the house in the night.

She moved forward stiffly, brain racing through explanations for what she was seeing, and discarding each one at once. She saw the window in the wall rise to meet her as she drew closer to it. She saw rhythmic movement behind the window.

The phone rang, and in the fraction of a second that it took to register on her brain, the brick wall dissolved, as if it were constructed of a dark and incredibly thin ice that hot sunlight had fallen upon.

She gasped, backed away from her window, toward the phone, which rang a second time, and shook her head quickly, her eyes now on a line of dark clouds at the eastern horizon that were tinged with red from the morning sun.

She reached back, grabbed the receiver, put it down, returned to the window. She studied the line of gray clouds, and tried hard to make of it what she had seen moments before.

Behind her, the phone rang again. She ignored it.

The man often carried a shotgun when he went walking in the woods, regardless of whether it was hunting season, but today he had left it home. He was merely walking, and thinking about Katherine and about what he had seen of her earlier that morning, when she'd come to her window naked. Damned good-looking woman. Enough to make a man think twice about other women.

He had decided that Katherine—whose name he had heard in reference to Jason's murder—hadn't known he was watching. After all, when a person buys a house on twenty-eight acres, she expects a bit of privacy. But it had been quite nice to watch her, and it was quite nice remembering her, now.

The man came to a narrow brook and stepped over it. He stopped and squinted through the fifty feet of woods remaining, at the fields beyond. He saw a dim, moving darkness, as if a soft black rain were falling. He glanced up, through the trees, at the deep blue sky. He lowered his gaze. He didn't like what he was seeing. It unnerved him and gnawed at his sense of the order of things—dark rain simply didn't fall from a cloudless blue sky. The idea spooked him and he devised quick, rational explanations for what he was seeing, all of which satisfied him and eased his anxiety.

Kennedy Whelan parked his Crown Victoria in front of Katherine's house, shut off the ignition, and fished in his suit pockets for a cigar. He had none. "Damn!" he whispered. The cigar was important. It was a prop, an agitation, it annoyed people, and when people were annoyed, they became incautious, so they made mistakes. Whelan was a self-styled student of human nature. He did not maintain that people were always easy to read. Sometimes, they were all but impossible to read. The young man who's just killed his best friend with a hammer might be telling jokes and asking for something to eat a half hour later. The woman who's thrown her child off a bridge might go straightaway to the beauty parlor. A lot of that kind of behavior was denial, of course. The deed is done, nothing can retrieve it or undo it, so as a way of wishing it away, of trivializing it, life gets lived—the meals get eaten, the toe-nails clipped, the baths taken, the soap operas watched. It was, he told himself, just the kind of behavior that Katherine Nichols had been engaging in, except that she had guilt layered onto guilt—an incestuous relationship with her brother, then his murder. (Whelan thought he knew very well what guilt could do, having hated his homosexuality for so long and having covered it up with macho bullshit for just as long. It made it that much easier to see the guilt in others.) So, she had been acting erratically because that double burden of guilt had put her off balance, like a spinning top that's had a couple of handfuls of mud slung at it.

He pushed his car door open, got out, started down the weathered fieldstone walkway toward the house. He stopped, aware that someone was watching him from one of the second-floor windows from behind a drawn curtain. He could see that the curtain was parted a little; he could see the tips of someone's fingers.

The front door of the house opened. Katherine stepped out onto the porch. She was dressed in her red, knee-length, terry cloth robe, which she had gathered tightly around herself. She said, her tone crisp, "What do you want, Mr. Whelan?"

He took several steps forward, so he was standing at the bottom of the steps. It was another ploy—if she was physically above him, then she might feel intellectually above him, too. And that would make her incautious. He shoved his hands into his pants pockets, raised his head to look at her, so his chin was sticking out. "I tried to call you earlier, Katherine—"

"You may not call me 'Katherine,' " she cut in.

He smiled a pretended apology. "I'm sorry. Miss Nichols. I tried to call you, but someone picked up the phone, then put it down again. Was that you?"

She didn't answer at once. She pursed her lips, then said, "Yes, it was me."

He smiled. "Are you in the habit of doing that?"

"No."

He said nothing for a long moment, his smile stuck on his face, his massive jaw continuing to jut out; then he lowered his head so he was looking at the first porch step. "I wanted to discuss your brother's case with you a bit more, Miss Nichols."

"I thought I'd made it clear that I had nothing more to say."

"You made that very clear." He looked at her again. He was still smiling, but it was a tighter smile now. "And I promise not to take up a lot of your time."

She said nothing.

"May we go inside?"

"No. If you have something to say, you can say it out here."

"Oh? Are you entertaining?"

"Entertaining?"

"A houseguest."

"I have no houseguests, Mr. Whelan."

"Of course not." A brief pause, then, "I wanted to ask you about your father." He saw her body stiffen and her face tighten. Whelan continued, "Do you mind if we talk about him?"

"I *mind* having to talk to you at all, Mr. Whelan."

He mounted the steps slowly and stopped on the step just below Katherine. He patted his pockets, again in search of a cigar, remembered that he had none, took the final step, and gestured at the dark wicker chairs on the porch. "May I sit down?"

"What did you want to ask about my father?" Katherine asked, ignoring his question.

He walked around in back of her and sat in the nearest chair. He stared at his car as he talked. "I wanted you to confirm or deny some reports I've received about him."

"I really do not understand—"

"Reports that he was charged with assault, Miss Nichols."

"Damn you!" Her voice was taut with anger.

"Then you're not denying that charges were filed?"

"It's a matter of public record. Of course I'm not denying it."

"Yes, it is a matter of public record. Can you tell me, then, *who* made the charges? Was it you?"

"You know it wasn't."

"Of course I do. It was your brother, wasn't it?"

"I think we've talked quite enough, Mr. Whelan." The anger was leaving her, Whelan thought, and something was replacing it—resolve. He pushed on. "Because it was your brother, it was *Jason* who was the victim of the assault, wasn't it?"

She said nothing.

"He found you—your father found you and Jason together, isn't that right? In your bedroom. Naked. And he nearly killed your brother. Isn't *that* right?"

"No," she whispered. "It isn't." She was whimpering; it pleased Whelan.

"As you said, Miss Nichols, it's all a matter of public record—"

She cut in hotly, "In this case, Mr. Whelan, the goddamned *public record* is wrong! Now will you please leave!"

He looked up at her. He said nothing. Her outburst had surprised him.

"Leave!" she repeated.

He stood, took several quick steps over to her, looked her squarely in the eye, and smiled a tight, threatening smile. "I just wanted you to know that I was still alive." And he went briskly to his car, got in, and drove away.

Anger stayed with Katherine for a long while. She went back inside, first to the living room, where she stood very erect behind one of the chairs and hit the top of it rhythmically with her fist, then into the kitchen, where she had fixed a bowl of dry cereal and a glass of orange juice just before Whelan's arrival. She sipped the juice and dumped the cereal out. Then she went upstairs to the bedroom she and Larry shared, where she got into her work clothes—jeans, a blue flannel shirt, a pair of loafers—then outside with her easel, a blank canvas, some brushes and oils.

She went north a hundred feet, toward the stand of woods, stopped, turned, and set up her easel and canvas. She would do a landscape today. The light was good—the low clouds from earlier in the morning had dissipated and the scene had a good, stiff, sunlit look to it that appealed to her. She'd decided to work in oils because it would be a change from the past few days, when she'd done a half dozen quick charcoal sketches of the house from various angles, none of which had pleased her. "They all look so unfinished," she had said to Larry, and he had nodded a little, making it clear that he had no idea what she was talking about. "You don't know what I mean, do you, Larry?"

"No," he answered. "Tell me."

"Tell you what I mean by 'unfinished'?"

"Yes."

She thought a moment, then conceded, "I don't really think I know, either. 'Incomplete,' I guess." And from there, the discussion had rapidly come to an end.

Today, she told herself, she'd do better. Oils were superior to charcoal, of course. She got realism from oils. That was their purpose. She didn't get it from charcoal. And realism was what she wanted, wasn't it? (She didn't forget Whelan or his questions. She wondered through her slowly dissolving anger what he meant when he asked if she was entertaining "a houseguest," but tucked his entire visit away with the idea that she'd talk to Larry about it. Maybe. Although he had never been particularly understanding about anyone in her family, especially Jason and her father.)

She'd been working for an hour and a half, painting precisely what she could see, and transferring it precisely to the canvas. She liked what she'd done. The quack grass—very tall and brown and sunlit—came way up the canvas, and as it came up it came forward, too, which gave it an animated look. It was thinner at the top than at the bottom, so, near the top, the blue sky cut sharply into it. She had no background, yet, though she could see the small stand of woods through the quack grass. She was thinking of adding it somehow. She had her brush poised an inch from the canvas, when she heard the voice of a child nearby; *"Mia madre,"* it said. And Katherine said, "Hello?" and added, after a moment, "Is someone there?" then listened. She heard the quack grass rustling close by. She looked. "Hello?" she said again, and saw, just inside the perimeter of the tall grass, what could have been a wide fringe of dark hair on a small, oval face, and large, dark eyes.

She said, "Hello," and added, "little girl." She put it together. "Hello, little girl."

The stiff rustling sound in the quack grass receded and she heard only the sound of her feet shuffling uneasily.

She put a little girl in her painting that day. A girl with long, dark hair, and large, dark, expressive eyes. She put her back a bit in the painting—in the quack grass, so she wasn't much more than the suggestion of a little girl. She thought it gave the painting a nice, comfortable look; children should play in the quack grass.

She said to Larry that night, as she watched him prepare supper, "I saw a little girl out back today. While I was painting."

Larry looked up from rolling a chicken drumstick in his own homemade breading. "Really? What was she doing there?"

Katherine shrugged. "God knows. All she said was something about her mother."

"Something about her mother? What does that mean?" He held the chicken drumstick up and studied it critically, grimaced, breathed a curse, and shoved it back into the breading.

"She was speaking in Italian," Katherine answered. "She said, *'Mia madre.'* That has something to with 'mother,' doesn't it?"

"Sure," Larry answered. "That's what *'madre'* means. 'Mother.' " He studied the chicken drumstick once more, looked pleased. "You want to make the coleslaw, Katherine?"

"I despise coleslaw. You know that."

He looked offended. "It's part of this meal," he said. "This meal is shit without coleslaw."

"It'll be shit with it, Larry. Why don't we have a salad? I like salad."

"I was looking forward to coleslaw." His voice had taken on a petulant tone. "Now, if you're not going to make it, *I* will."

She raised an eyebrow. "Lighten up, Larry. I'll make the damned coleslaw."

"Thanks." His voice still had a petulant edge to it. He went on, his tone gentler, as if in apology, "*'Mia madre'* means 'my mother.' The little girl was looking for her mother."

Chapter Twenty-nine

He was a first-time hiker, and he was exhausted. It was several days after Whelan's visit to Katherine; dusk and the light were failing.

The hiker's name was Tim Lowe, twenty-nine, a technical writer who smoked too much, had the beginnings of emphysema moving into his lungs—though he wasn't aware of it—and he was hiking on a bet. If he finished the hike, which had begun thirty-five miles east of where he was now, and ended twenty-five miles north, in Jefferson—then he'd get to spend a lively weekend with his vivacious coworker, Janice.

"You want to get it on with me, Tim," she had told him, "then you've got to be pretty fucking fit," which was a phrase that made her chuckle. "Hell, Tim, you think I want you falling dead right in the middle of it?"

So he had eagerly accepted the challenge. He

bought himself a good pair of hiking boots—
which had proved, painfully, to be half a size too
small—and a backpack that he'd filled with all
the right "hiker's foods"—Hershey bars, peanut
butter, hunter's bread—and he had even left his
cigarettes at home.

A path had already been mapped out for him,
by Janice and some of her friends. It bisected a
few roads, but paralleled none, which was to
help ensure that he didn't cheat. A small section
of the path led through the woods a half mile
behind Katherine's house. It was there, in those
woods, that Tim decided to rest.

Because there seemed to be no area on his
body that didn't ache, he clumsily took off his
backpack, then his boots, and he lay on a soft
bed of pine needles.

He woke, reluctantly, at a little past 11:00
P.M., pulling himself out of a dream about Janice
and what he was going to do with her on their
own "special weekend." It was a dream he had
had more than once, with many variations, and
this time he'd employed them all.

He sat up on the bed of pine needles and felt
around for his backpack. He found it, opened it,
fished inside, and found a Hershey bar, which he
ate ravenously.

Night was a good time for walking, he'd been

told. It was cooler, there was more oxygen in the air. Of course, you had to watch where you were going, and that was difficult for him, especially here. He put his boots on, stood, slipped into the backpack, and noted with relief that his various aches and pains had lessened.

"What is your name?" he heard from close by. He lurched forward a few steps because the voice had startled him and his brain and muscles had told him to run. But he stopped, turned toward the voice—certain that it was just a farmer trying to keep trespassers away—and said, "I'm sorry."

The voice repeated, with urgency, "What is your name?"

Tim couldn't see well at night—a vitamin A deficiency, poor diet—but he thought he could make out an oblong, darkish form several feet away, so he said again, "I'm sorry," then added, "I didn't see any Posted signs."

"What is your name?" the voice repeated, and Tim watched as the oblong form moved a couple of feet closer.

"My name's Tim Lowe," Tim said.

And the oblong form said, "I love you, Tim."

"Larry?" Katherine said. They were in the living room, both naked, lying close to one another on the hardwood floor. They had just made love and it had been a chore for them both—Katherine because images of her brother came to her again and again; images from their childhood together, their last few moments, and she had been unable to push them away—and Larry because it had been clear to him that her mind was elsewhere and it annoyed him.

"Yes?" he said.

"That man was here the other day."

"What man?"

"That cop. Whelan. He wanted to talk to me about my father."

"Christ!" Larry thought he had a good idea now what had been on her mind during their lousy lovemaking. "Christ," he repeated, "do you have to bring that up now?"

"He wanted to know what—"

Larry interrupted, "I'd rather not talk about it, okay!"

"And what if *I* do?"

"Then you'll have to talk to someone else. That whole thing makes me sick."

"It was a picnic for me, Larry. I enjoy talking about it." She pushed herself stiffly to her feet. "Goddammit, where's my robe?"

"You understand, don't you?" Larry asked from the floor.

"No," she answered. "I don't understand.

Goddammit, it was my father and *my* problem."

"Katherine, please."

"And *you're* the one who gets squeamish." She glanced furiously around the dark room. "Where the fuck is my robe?"

"Of course I'm squeamish about it. My God, Jason had problems—you can't deny it."

"No," she said. "He did not have *problems,* Larry."

"I could see it in him. I didn't want to admit it, for your sake—"

"Have I ever pleaded with you before, Larry?" Her voice had a chilling air of forced calm about it.

"Pleaded with me? I don't understand."

"I'm pleading with you now. Don't talk to me about Jason."

"Sure, Katherine. But do you know what it sounds like? It sounds like you're running from something. I don't know, like you're hiding from something." He paused, then added, "Katherine, I've got to ask this, I've got to know: Did you kill him? Did you kill Jason?"

She found her robe, shrugged stiffly into it, turned away from him.

"Katherine?" Larry said.

She left the room, went to the foyer, to the front door, pulled it open.

221

"Katherine? It was just a question. I'm interested, that's all."

She stepped out onto the porch, looked right, left. Then she ran off the porch, around the house, into the fields. Behind her, at the kitchen door, Larry called, "I just wanted to know, Katherine. That's all. Chill out, okay? Hey, I'll put some coffee on."

It was the developing emphysema that helped to kill Tim Lowe. The heavy, moist night air helped, as well. So did fear. His death took several minutes, and a couple of times while it was happening, he felt that he would come out of it all right, which made him thankful, so he uttered small, grateful prayers, though he had never been particularly religious. He also made major resolutions about changing the course of his life if he did indeed survive.

He lost consciousness in the midst of one of these resolutions, then regained it, smiling and happy that he could no longer feel the heavy grip of a hand on the back of his head, and couldn't smell the strong odors of cloves and starch. And could not hear the voice, which said again and again, "I love you, Tim Lowe." But it was only a short-lived respite. The hand returned, and the smells. And the voice. And as he slipped off, finally and forever, he heard another voice, farther off:

> *"Good night? ah! no; the hour is ill*
> *Which severs those it should unite;*
> *Let us remain together still,*
> *Then it will be good night."*

If it had not been happening to him, Tim Lowe might have thought that there were worse ways to die than to slip into an oxygen-deprived sleep while an anonymous voice recited Keats.

It was several minutes before Katherine realized what she had done, that she'd run from the house, from Larry and his questions and suspicions. And when at last she did realize it, and had stopped running, she was halfway to the trees, halfway to the dying Tim Lowe, and was unaware of where she was, precisely, because the weeds around her were very tall.

Her head cleared slowly. This took several minutes of talking out loud to herself in the blackness and the tall weeds: "No, Larry really doesn't believe that you killed Jason. No, he didn't mean to ask what he asked. He asked it because he was concerned, and that's his way, he's just *clumsy.* . . ." And, "No one would kill

Jason. He was too kind, too gentle. He had no problems. He was human. He loved me, that's all. That was his only sin. He was too human. He loved me and he had his own off-key way of showing it. Always. His own way. Who can blame him for that?" Then back to, "No, Larry really doesn't believe you killed Jason. He didn't mean to ask it, no. . . ." Which finally convinced her that she had, after all, to go back to her house, that it would do her no good to stay out here. So she started back, and realized within moments that she had no idea which way to go. There was no moon and a mantle of low clouds had moved in on a sudden breeze. She thought, *This is country living; you find out about darkness.* It was an attempt to chase her fear away, because it was tugging hard at her, trying to pull her in all directions at once, because there was safety in movement, anyway. "This is country living," she said aloud. "You find out what darkness is." The sound of her own voice calmed her. She looked right, then left, then behind. She saw that she was in a shallow depression, which was why the weeds seemed so tall. Close to her—she reached out and touched them—they were only waist-high. If she moved up and out of the depression, she'd be able to see the house. She did it. She stopped. The first thought that came to her as an explanation for what she was seeing here was that she had run much farther than she'd thought, and that the huge brick house in front of her was some anonymous farmhouse far beyond her property, and that it had been abandoned long ago, which would explain why there were no lights on inside it, and why the tall weeds hugged it so tightly.

She saw a large, still form in one of the lower windows. Vaguely, she saw pale flesh and a mound of dark hair, the suggestion of eyes and mouth.

"I'm sorry," she whispered. "I didn't mean to bother you."

The form nodded once, and Katherine became aware that it was leaning forward, so its hands were on the inside of the windowsill, supporting its body.

Katherine moved toward the house, her steps slow and deliberate. The sharp edges of the weeds dragged across the backs of her hands as she moved, and she was aware that the ground here was very soft, as if from a recent heavy rain. She sensed warmth from the house, and friendship, despite its size and the darkness.

It was the house's front porch that she was walking to. It was a wide, wraparound porch, and the brick steps were worn, though not crumbling.

She saw two dark house numbers on one of the wooden columns supporting the porch roof. They were the numbers 2 and 6. It seemed odd that this house should be number 26, without a road nearby, or any other houses, for that matter. Number 2600, perhaps, but not number 26. Then she saw that there was a space between the two numbers, and she decided that the number was actually something like 216 or 226, which made more sense.

She climbed the steps and called, "Hello," as if, she thought, she were a Welcome Wagon hostess.

She crossed the porch to the front door; it was huge, apparently made of oak, and it sported rectangular leaded glass inserts and a lion's-head brass door knocker. She used the knocker and called again, "Hello?"

A light went on deep within the first floor of the house. Probably the kitchen, she thought. She peered through the windows in the front door. Another light winked on. A hall light. The hall led to the kitchen.

"Hello?" she called again, and added, "Is anyone there, please?"

A light in the foyer came on, though she could

see no one, only the foyer, which was bare of furniture, the long hallway, also bare, and the kitchen at the end of the hallway, which had a small wooden dining set in it.

She realized that she was smiling. She put her eye to the window in the front door and saw what at first looked like a painting on one of the foyer walls—the portrait of a woman with a round and cheerful face, whose eyes were small and crowded by puffs of fat. An odd sort of painting, she thought. Then the eyes opened wide, the mouth moved, and she jerked backward and stood bolt upright in surprise.

The woman behind the door pushed it open and stuck her head out. "I'm so sorry," she gushed. She was dressed in a huge red terry cloth robe. "I didn't want to scare you, miss. Did I scare you?"

"No," Katherine said. "You surprised me. I didn't know anyone was living here. I didn't even know this *house* was here. I live"—she nodded to her left, thinking as she did it that she could just as easily have nodded in any direction because she had no real idea where her house was— "over there. I just moved in a few weeks ago."

"Yes," the woman said. She still had only her round head stuck out the door and she was smiling a big, warm smile. "I know that."

227

Katherine liked the woman's voice. It was a low tenor, a little pinched-sounding, probably because of the rolls of fat around her throat. But it was a friendly voice, and caring.

Katherine said, "I'm Katherine Nichols," and stuck her hand out.

The woman said, "I know that, too," stared a moment at Katherine's hand, then stuck her massive left arm around the doorway and touched the tips of Katherine's fingers. It was like the touch of a butterfly. "Forgive me," she said, "but I am not ready yet, you see, to receive visitors. Not just yet." And she closed the door. Within moments, the three lights that had been turned on inside the big house winked out. Katherine pressed her face into the window. She could see nothing at all, not even the suggestion of walls and doors within the house, as if blindness began there, just beyond the door.

"Hello?" she called. "Hello?" She stepped back. She listened. Behind her, she heard some night creature slip through the tall weeds. Around her, she imagined that she could feel the house vibrating very slightly, as if the big woman inside were moving about. But she knew at once that she felt nothing, that the massive house was still, as if it were indeed just a long-abandoned farmhouse, as she had first supposed.

228

She found herself backing slowly down the porch steps. The warmth that she'd felt here minutes earlier was gone. Now the house was just an obstruction on the landscape, and ugly, too—as, surely, the woman inside it had been. Massive and ugly. An intrusion. An intruder! Damn it, goddammit, what in the hell was it *doing* here?

"What in the hell is it doing here?" she whispered. The sound of her own voice gave her no comfort. It sounded desperate and weak. It sounded like the voice of someone falling. *Hang on tight, sis!*

She backed away from the house and into the waist-high weeds around it. She did not take her eyes off it, but she lost it, anyway, as the weeds crowded around her and flooded into her foreground, and the dark red bricks flowed back into the darkness.

Larry gave her a cup of coffee when she got home. It was lukewarm because it had been sitting in the pot over the pilot light for almost an hour. He led her to a chair in the kitchen and waited for her to speak. She didn't.

He said, "I almost came out looking for you," as if that would have been some great and noble

229

sacrifice and wasn't she grateful that he'd even considered it?

She said, looking down at her cup of coffee, "No. I was okay. I just had some trouble getting my bearings."

"I'm sorry we fought," he said. He was seated opposite her at the small table. He leaned back in his chair and clasped his hands behind his head. "And I'm sorry if I said anything that upset you. I was trying to be honest. I guess I was trying to get *you* to be honest, Katherine."

She looked up at him with confusion. "I don't know what that means," she said. "Really. I don't know what that means. I have no secrets from you. Whatever you *should* know about me, you do know."

"But who makes that determination, Katherine? Who decides what I *should* know and what I shouldn't know?"

"I do, of course."

"Then it's possible, isn't it, that you could have secrets—"

"If I do, they don't *mean* anything. My God, I never realized before how much you mistrusted me."

"Katherine, I don't mistrust *you*, I mistrust . . ." He leaned forward over the table so he was closer to her. He went on, his voice a conspiratorial whisper, "I mistrust the person *inside* you. I don't know that person. I don't think *you* know her."

Katherine said nothing.

Larry coaxed, "Katherine? Do you know what I'm saying?"

Still nothing.

"Katherine?"

She pushed her chair away from the table suddenly, spilling some of the coffee. She stared at the spill a moment, stood, looked at Larry, who was still sitting. Her mouth moved a little, but she said nothing. Then she looked at the spill— *It was so ugly! Hang on tight, sis!*—rounded the table, and started for the living room. She stopped. "Clean that up, would you?" she said, and nodded at the spill. *It was so ugly! . . . Of course it was ugly.* "Please," she went on.

"Sure," Larry answered. "No problem. Where are you going?"

"To bed," she told him. "I'm very tired." And she left the room.

Chapter Thirty

Bill Straub found Tim Lowe's body two mornings later, while he was running his usual route—down the west side of Katherine's property, past the line of poplars, and through the stand of woods. It was, in fact, the same path that Tim Lowe had used.

Bill spotted the body easily. It was just off the path, lying facedown, arms and legs spread, face turned to the left. Tim's eyes and mouth were half open. A large and colorful garden spider had constructed a massive and beautiful web between Tim's chin—which sported a two-day growth of beard—and the lower branches of a sapling fir nearby. Several deerflies had been trapped in the web, one quite recently, because it was buzzing frantically in a futile attempt to free itself.

Bill Straub stared at Tim for a long while; finally, he said, "You're dead, aren'cha?" It occurred to him at that moment that he had never seen a dead body before. He thought that if someone had asked him what his reaction would be if he found a dead man in the woods, he'd have said that he'd for sure keep away from the dead man, and that he'd for sure not look at the dead man's face, and that he would for sure not touch him.

He hadn't touched him, but he was finding that the dead man's face was awfully interesting. He thought he had never seen a face before that was anything like it. A department store dummy's face was almost like it, he thought, but it wasn't exactly the same. A department store dummy's face had always been a department store dummy's face. It never had tears running down its cheeks, and it never had its mouth open to scream, and it had never slept. This poor dead face had done all those things.

And Bill thought, as well, that the man's death had been easy. He didn't know why. Maybe because it didn't look like the man had been in a fight, or that someone had shot him or knifed him or hit him with an axe or a baseball bat. He just looked like he'd died all of a sudden and fallen flat on his face.

Bill turned from Tim Lowe's body, then, and

jogged back, the way he'd come, up the path, toward Katherine's house, because it had occurred to him all at once that he had an absolutely perfect excuse, now, to hang around her for a while. Her husband (if that's what he was) was gone. And even if she called him, it would take him a long time to drive back, because the rumor was that he worked in the city. And if she called the cops (well, she was going to have to do that, of course), then he'd still have to hang around because *he'd* found the dead man's body, after all.

Katherine was on her back porch setting up her easel. She was looking forward to her work today. She was thinking that in the past few days, she had grown to feel very much at home here. Not with the house, particularly, though it was comfortable enough (especially when she was alone in it, and, because Larry commuted every day, she had more than a few hours alone in it), but more with the land itself. And, oddly, Jason's terrible death and burial hadn't put a blot on it. That seemed outside it, somehow. As if the land had been violated, yes, but was healing nicely. As she was. When spring came, she would have no trouble at all starting a patch of vegetables in the garden where Jason's killer had put him.

And, of course, his was not the first death that had happened here. There was the previous owner, whose death had apparently been quick and natural. And others, too. Those that still were missing, as well as those who had lived in the house before it was moved here. *A place that's good to die in,* she thought, *has to be a place that's good to live in, too.*

She had trouble setting up the easel. One of the leg bolts was stuck and she had to use a good deal of strength to turn it; she cursed with the effort. It was as she was cursing that she felt the porch floor vibrate through the soles of her feet, as if someone else were on it, and she turned her head and looked. Bill Straub was at the opposite end of the porch; he was bent over so his hands were on his knees-and his head was down. He was breathing heavily; she could see that he'd been running hard. "Miss Nichols . . ." he managed, and took a deep breath. "Miss Nichols, someone . . ."

She went over to him, reached out as if to comfort him, decided against it. "What is it, Bill?"

He nodded toward the stand of woods. "A guy's . . . dead over there!"

She stepped away from him, stiffened.

"Over there," Bill said. "In the woods!"

"Who is it?" Katherine whispered.

236

Bill shook his head, then looked up at her. "I don't know. You better not go back there, though. It ain't a pretty sight."

Katherine closed her eyes. *Hang on tight, sis!*

Bill went on, with great urgency, "Dead man ain't pretty things, Miss Nichols!" He was catching his breath. He straightened and took a few slow steps toward her.

She still had her eyes closed. *It was so ugly! It was so ugly! And Jason wasn't ugly!*

"You think," Bill went on, "you might know him, Miss Nichols?"

"No, Bill," she said, "I'm sure I don't." She turned from him to go back into the house. Her shoulder grazed the unsteady easel and it clattered to the porch floor. She looked at it, startled. "Damn it!" she whispered. "Goddammit!" and went quickly inside. Bill followed.

She went to the phone, dialed the sheriff's office. "Mr. Busher," she said, "this is Katherine Nichols. You'll have to come out here, right away."

She watched Bill cross the kitchen to her, watched him put his hands on her shoulders. "It's okay, Miss Nichols," he breathed. "I'm here!"

"Get your hands off me!" she snapped.

Bill stepped away from her. He was trembling. "Gee, Miss Nichols. I'm sorry."

"Yes," she said in a response to Busher. She paused, then said, "I believe there's been another murder."

Chapter Thirty-one

She was sitting in the kitchen when Larry got home that evening at a little past 8:00. She had a cup, drained of coffee, in front of her; her hands were around it, and when Larry came in she looked up at him and gave him a quivering smile.

"Hi," she said.

He crossed the room, kissed her softly on the cheek, looked about. "I was kind of hoping you'd have some dinner ready for me, Katherine. Were you working today?" It had been agreed recently that on days she painted they would each see to the preparation of their own meals, but that on days when she chose to be idle she would make dinner for them both. Weekends were split between them.

"No," she answered. "I didn't work today."

He went to a cupboard, opened it, found a few

cans of vegetables, a can of tuna. He opened another cupboard, found it all but empty, too. "I guess we're going to have shop soon," he said.

"Yes, we are."

A slip of yellow paper on the counter caught his eye; he picked it up, read it: "What's this?"

She looked at him. He was holding it out to her. "It's a bill," she said.

He glanced at it again. "Who's this 'Kennedy Whelan'?"

"He's the cop who was investigating Jason's death. I burned his suit. It was an accident. That's the bill for fixing it."

"Burned his suit. How in hell did you—"

"He came over today."

"Why? To bring you this?" He was incredulous.

"No." She looked away.

"Katherine?" he coaxed.

"They found a body," she said. "Out there, in the woods."

"Jesus, and you didn't call me?"

"Why would I?"

"I don't know. So I could come home and *be* here with you. To comfort you."

She shrugged. "I think I preferred being alone."

"You preferred being alone?"

"It had nothing to do with you, Larry."

He said nothing. He looked perplexed, hurt, a little angry.

Katherine said, "They think this man died of natural causes. That's what Whelan told me."

Larry was still holding Whelan's bill. He folded it now, with slow precision, once, then again, and again, so it was a small square piece of yellow paper, which he shoved into his pants pocket. He looked very puzzled. He glanced toward the rear of the house, then toward the entrance to the kitchen, then at Katherine, who was looking into her empty cup. "This is all very strange . . ." He stopped, uncertain how to continue.

Katherine said, still looking into her cup, "No, it isn't, Larry. People die every day. This man died near the house. There's nothing strange about that. Not really."

"You should have called me. I'd prefer that you had called me," Larry said.

"I didn't need comforting."

"Everyone needs comforting from time to time, Katherine."

"And you would have just been in the way."

"Oh, for Christ's sake!"

"It wasn't that important. Someone died. People die every day."

"Yes, you said that."

She grinned. She was still looking into her coffee cup. "I did, didn't I?" She sounded vaguely amused. "I'll make you some dinner if you'd like. We have chicken. You like chicken."

"I don't want any chicken."

She looked admonishingly at him. "Please don't be angry with me." She looked away. "You told me you'd change if we got back together and I'd like to think you were being sincere. I'd like to think you weren't giving me another line of bullshit."

"What does that have to do with what happened here today?"

"A lot. It has a lot to do with it. You go on and on"—she was starting to gesticulate wildly—"about wanting to *be* here, to *comfort* me. I don't need comforting, Larry. I don't need it, not by you—I just don't need it!" She paused to collect her thoughts, then turned her head and looked very sternly at him. "I need to be myself. I need peace. And quiet. Peace and quiet. Can you appreciate that?"

"Yes. I can appreciate it." He had little idea what to say to her. "I was just going to tell you that I'm really . . . blameless . . ." He grinned bemusedly, then repeated, "Really blameless . . ."

Katherine murmured, "Yes, you are." She was

looking into her empty cup again. "It upset me, Larry." She was speaking in tight whispers now, as if trying hard to control herself. "It reminded me of Jason."

"Of course it did. I can understand that." He came over, stood behind her, and began massaging her shoulders. "I can understand that," he repeated.

"I've just been sitting here all afternoon, Larry. Right here at this table. Drinking coffee. Thinking."

"You won't be able to sleep."

"Sure I will."

Chapter Thirty-two

She woke very early the following morning, well before dawn. She woke because she had been sleeping fitfully the entire night, sliding in and out of dreams that were cold and claustrophobic, the kind that fever usually brings. She stayed awake because she sensed something in the smooth country darkness around her.

She sat up in bed and glanced at Larry, sleeping on his side, facing away from her (he had tried to make love to her while she slept, but she had shooed him away). She got out of bed quietly, not wanting to wake him, and stood near the bed, listening. She heard from below the slight, brittle noise of glass striking glass. It was a noise she had heard more than once at the house, and she thought now that it was really quite pleasant.

She also heard, distantly, what could have

245

been the hum of a car engine. She let her gaze linger on the window and saw that a couple of moths had settled onto the screen, that one was moving about, and she thought it was odd she could see them with such clarity, as if they were backlit.

In his sleep, Larry mumbled an incoherency, scratched his elbow, fell silent. Katherine glanced at him, made a small, shushing gesture with her hand, and found at the same time that she was smiling, as if she were about to experience something pleasant and didn't want Larry to interrupt it.

She moved quickly to the window, leaned over, put her hands on the sill.

She recognized the large woman looking up at her and her smile broadened in greeting. Then she saw that there were other people clustered around the woman—a tall, scruffy boy, a young, dark-haired woman, a small child, perhaps a girl (it was difficult to tell in the darkness), and her smile became a look of inquiring and friendly confusion. *Who are your friends?* it said.

Behind her, Larry mumbled another incoherency. She shushed him again.

And below, she saw that the half dozen people who had been clustered together looking up at her were drifting off.

246

Then she saw the houses—warm, geometrical swellings in the early morning darkness, barely recognizable from the land itself, as if they had sprung from it.

It was into these houses that the fat woman and the scruffy boy, the small child and the others were disappearing. Katherine watched them go, watched lights come on inside the houses, watched their inhabitants move about inside, heard the murmur of voices talking contentedly, smelled the street itself, a city street alive with city smells.

Then she watched the morning light break in and wash the houses away.

And behind her, Larry's alarm clock sounded and she turned from the window, went over, and shut the clock off.

Larry woke, looked at her. "Hi," he said.

"Hi," she said, smiling. "I'll make you some breakfast, if you'd like."

"Sure." He was pleased. "What's the occasion?" He sat up on the edge of the bed.

She sat on the bed with him, turned her head, looked at him, smiled a slight smile. "Friendship," she said.

Chapter Thirty-three

Kennedy Whelan had few illusions about himself. He knew that he was overweight and that he had never been particularly good to look at—although he dressed well—that he had a foul and unpredictable temper, and that his breath smelled of cigar smoke and coffee. But he knew also that he was pretty damned bright, and he knew that other people knew it, too. Katherine Nichols knew it. He was sure of that.

Problem was, she thought she was even brighter. That was obvious. Otherwise she wouldn't be playing games with him; she'd have tried to run, to lose herself, because he would have spooked her.

But she hadn't run. And that meant, of course, that she thought she was brighter than he. And although it was possible that somewhere in this world there was a woman who *was* brighter,

Katherine Nichols was simply not that woman. She didn't even come close. She made too many mistakes.

He brought his car to a slow, easy stop in front of her house, leaned over, gave the house a long once-over. It was early afternoon, three days after Tim Lowe's murder, and he had brought Katherine the county medical examiner's Final Report of Autopsy. There was nothing impressive or condemning about it. It noted only that *the deceased probably died of natural causes complicated by developing emphysema,* but it was an excellent prop, and chances were good that it would get him into the house.

It did.

Katherine showed him into the living room and pointed at a delicate, light oak rocking chair. "Sit there, please," she said. He sat in it. She sat across the room from him, in her white wicker chair, hands folded on her knees. She said nothing, which unnerved Whelan, because he was convinced that letting her talk first would give him the upper hand.

He said, trying hard to sound casual, "I have the autopsy report on Tim Lowe's murder. I thought you'd like to see it, Katherine." He grinned.

"Why would I want to see it?" she asked.

He pretended a quick chuckle, as if seeing through her charade, pulled the report from an inside pocket of his suit, unfolded it, and pretended to read it. "It says something interesting, Katherine."

"I doubt that."

Again a quick chuckle. "It says—"

"Don't call me Katherine," she interrupted. "Only my friends call me Katherine."

He nodded. "Of course." Another glance at the report. "It says that Tim Lowe 'probably' died of natural causes."

"Congratulations." She was stone-faced.

"Congratulations?"

"Yes. It confirms what you told me."

He thought a moment, remembered. "So it does," he said. "I was just guessing. An informed and educated guess. But I think the operative word in the report—"

"Is that all, Mr. Whelan?"

Her interruption took him by surprise, and it angered him. "No, that's not all!"

"Oh." Vague, unconcerned disappointment.

"It sure as hell is not all. I'm not here to do you any favors, Miss Nichols."

"I'm aware of that." She was still stone-faced.

"The operative word in the report"—he was

trying very hard to control his temper—"is this
word." He jabbed the report with his forefinger.
"'Probably.' Tim Lowe 'probably' died of natural
causes. 'Probably,' Miss Nichols!"

"Could you please get to the point, Mr. Whelan? I have a visitor."

"A visitor?" He grinned again. "A visitor?" he
repeated.

She stood abruptly. "Yes. And I think this conversation has run its course, don't you?"

Again she took him by surprise. He stood,
fished a cigar from his pocket, stuck it into his
mouth. "I just wanted you to know that I was
still alive, Miss Nichols."

"Yes," she said. "Of course you are."

He bit hard on the cigar and felt his fists clench
in anger. He took the cigar from his mouth,
crumbled it so bits of tobacco fell to the rug.
Then he quickly left the house.

Katherine went back into the kitchen, where
her visitor had been waiting. The kitchen was
empty, and she was not surprised. The visitor
had seemed tentative and uncertain—like blue
sky in February.

She could still smell the vague odor of her perspiration, and it was not unpleasant. It was very
human and honest.

She went to the back door, opened it, stepped

out onto the porch. She looked for her visitor but didn't see her, and that did not surprise her, either. Because the quack grass in the fields behind the house was tall and the visitor had been somewhat less than tall. If she was there, in one of the shallow depressions in the fields, she would be invisible.

Katherine hoped the visitor would come again soon. She had been good company, good to talk to, a comfort. And she was also the reason, Katherine knew, that Whelan had been so easy to deal with. She liked the idea that she'd gotten him angry, that he was seething with anger and unable to control himself. Let him feel the way she had so often been made to feel.

He'd be back, she knew, and that fact made her nervous. She became aware that her hands were shaking, that she was becoming light-headed.

"Gloria," she murmured. It was her visitor's name. A massive, comforting woman who had good things to say. But she'd be back, too, and that fact calmed Katherine. She turned and went into her house.

Part Three
Orchid Street

Chapter Thirty-four

Five days after the murder of Tim Lowe

They were having a picnic behind the house.

"Why are we doing this?" Larry asked, and waved at the blanket they'd laid out. He was trying to shoo some flies away. "It's too hot," he went on, "and these flies are going to eat us alive. They're deerflies, I think." He was sitting cross-legged on the edge of the blanket. "Deerflies bite. You know that, don't you?"

Katherine was lying on her side on the grass near him, her hand holding her head up. "Don't be a grump," she said. "How often do we get to do this, anyway?"

"Too often," he said.

"Jesus, Larry, picnics are *romantic* and *calming,* and"—she thought a moment—"and they're supposed to make you feel good. I thought you knew that."

"Sure I do. And they are romantic and calming, if you don't try to eat. I mean, they're peachy keen if you don't try to eat."

"I need this," she said.

He sighed. "I know you do." He fixed himself a plate of tuna salad and beans and repeated, "I know," and added, "I'm sorry."

She began, "These past few weeks have been awful—"

"I know that," he interrupted. "They've been awful for me, too." He pushed a forkful of tuna salad into his mouth, grimaced. "What kind of tuna is this?"

She shrugged. "I don't know. Bumble Bee, I think. It's Bumble Bee. Don't you like it?"

"It's too fishy." He put the plate on the blanket and stared at it as if it were something vile. "Maybe it's gone bad."

"It hasn't gone bad, Larry."

He sipped the lemonade, swallowed hard. "Jesus, it even makes the lemonade taste lousy."

"Larry, please—"

"And besides, don't you think *I've* been tense because of all the crap that's been going on? Huh?"

258

She didn't answer. She was trying to control her temper.

He pushed on. "This isn't the ideal situation for me, you know. I mean . . . I've got to get up before I'm even awake, for Christ's sake!"

"You invited yourself here, Larry. Remember that. I only said okay."

He stared at her a moment. "I'm not complaining, Katherine. I'm simply telling you what I feel. *I'm* here because *you're* here. . . ."

"My protector, you mean?"

He shrugged. "No, that's not what I mean, precisely. But now that you mention it—sure, why not?"

"I don't need your protection, Larry." She prepared a plate for herself, then made a show of enjoying the tuna.

He said, "Where do you go at night?"

"What?" She looked confused.

"I said where do you go at night? It's a simple question."

"I don't go anywhere at night. I go for walks."

"For walks?"

"Yes, I enjoy it. I go for little walks. It's very comforting. It's peaceful."

"Don't you think it disturbs me to wake up at God knows when, at two or three in the morning,

259

and find that you're not in bed? Don't you think that disturbs me?"

"I don't think it *concerns* you, Larry." She sighed, rushed on, "No, I'm sorry. It does concern you, doesn't it? It concerns both of us."

"Yes, it does." He glanced about. "Did you make anything except that foul tuna?"

"I don't think it's foul."

"Well, it is." He stuck his fork into his tuna, played with it a bit. "Where do you go on these walks of yours?"

She nodded to indicate the grassy fields. "Out there. I use the path that the Straub boy uses. It's nice. It's quiet and peaceful. It helps me think."

"You know there are bats out there at night."

She smiled. "I'm not concerned about bats."

"You know that ten percent of all bats are rabid, don't you? That's a pretty high percentage."

"I told you, Larry, I'm not concerned about the bats. Are you trying to spook me or something?"

"Spook you? Of course not. I'm just trying to alert you to some of the dangers—"

"Because I know about the bats. I hear them. I hear lots of things. I hear insects, and birds. I even hear people talking. But I don't get spooked, because I know that the bats aren't going to go after me, and I know that I don't really

260

hear people talking, because the nearest house is a mile away. You try to make yourself look superrational, Larry, and you end up looking like a fool."

"I just wish you'd think twice before you go on these walks again—"

"I'm old enough to make my own decisions. I don't like being bullied."

"I'm not bullying you. Jesus, Katherine, that's the second time you've used that word on me, and I'm beginning to resent it. A lot."

"Go ahead. Resent it."

He stood. "I'm going inside."

She closed her eyes and pursed her lips, annoyed. She opened her eyes, patted the blanket. "Oh, come on, Larry. Sit down. Eat. The tuna's good, the lemonade's good. Have a roll. I'll put some butter on it for you." She reached into the picnic basket and withdrew a hard roll, then looked around for the butter. Larry sat down again, with obvious reluctance. "Do you apologize, Katherine?"

"For what?" She continued looking for the butter.

"For calling me a fool."

She thought a moment, remembered using the word in passing. "Sure," she told him. "I apologize." She shoved the roll at him. "Now eat. Please."

He took the roll. "Did you find any butter in there?" He nodded at the picnic basket.

She looked another moment, then shook her head. "No, I'm sorry. Eat it that way. Butter's not good for you."

He split it open, ladled some of the tuna salad on it. "The bread will mask the taste," he said.

"Uh-huh," she said.

Chapter Thirty-five

One week after the murder of Tim Lowe

Katherine watched as a tall, thin man wearing a red and black hunting jacket moved with great deliberation across her backyard. He stopped several feet from her—she was at the bottom of the back porch steps—and grinned a big, ugly grin.

"Fine day," he said, "ain't it?"

She didn't answer.

"I said it's a fine day, ain't it?"

"Yes," she said.

"Fine day for walkin', wouldn't you say?"

"Yes."

"That's what I been doin'—I been walkin'."

"I know that," Katherine said. "I've been watching you."

His grin broadened. "Have you now? Why would you do that?"

"Sorry?"

"I say, why would you be watchin' me?"

Katherine shook her head once, slowly, as if confused. "I don't know. . . ."

"I'm pretty nice to look at, you think?"

Katherine didn't answer.

"I said, you think I'm pretty nice to look at?"

She nodded at the rifle slung over his shoulder. "I have signs up. . . ."

"Posted signs, you mean?"

"Yes." She was getting nervous.

"I didn't see none of 'em."

She stayed quiet; she wished he'd go away.

"I said I didn't see none of your Posted signs."

"I heard what you said."

"You got to put 'em up where people can see 'em, ya know. They metal ones?"

"No."

"Paper, then?"

"Yes, paper."

"Paper ones ain't worth shit. You got to get metal ones."

She nodded toward the woods. "Have you been hunting in there?"

His grin became a leer. "Not today, I ain't."

"I don't want you hunting in there. Please."

264

He let out a quick chuckle. "Sure enough. Hunting season don't start for a couple months, anyway."

She studied his face a moment, then asked, "Do I know you?" because she thought she recognized his voice.

The question surprised him. "You want to?" he said.

"No," she said.

His grin vanished, then reappeared. "You got something against huntin'?"

She nodded. "Yes, I do."

"You ever done it? You ever hunted?"

"Yes."

"What'd you hunt"

"I'd like you to leave now, please."

"You hunt deer? You hunt raccoon? Possum?"

She asked again, "Do I know you?" and noted a hint of urgency in her voice. "Were you one of the men looking for my brother?"

"Your brother? He missing?"

"He's dead."

"Is that right?" Katherine saw a little smile play across his mouth. "He the one that was murdered, was he?"

"Yes," she answered. "He was. And I'm not going to ask you again—I want you to leave!"

265

"How was he murdered? He get shot?"

"I'm going to go inside now, and I'm going to phone the police."

"The police?" He chuckled. "We ain't got no police here, miss. We got a deputy sheriff."

She turned halfway, started for the back door, then looked back. "What's your name?" she asked.

"Steamer, miss," he answered at once, and nodded as if in greeting. "Stanley Steamer. Pleased to make your acquaintance."

She turned again, quickly went to the back door, opened it. When she looked back, the man was gone.

"Sheriff Busher? This is Katherine Nichols."

"Yes, Miss Nichols, what is it?"

She took a breath, then said, "I'm not sure, but I think that hunter was here."

"What hunter?"

She fought back a sudden twinge of anger. "The one who called me. The one who shot my brother! *That* hunter!"

"Oh. Sorry. Of course." A brief pause. "You're calling from home?"

"Yes."

"And are you saying you'd like someone to

come out there and take your statement? Is that what you're saying?"

"For God's sake—"

"Because we're all pretty busy right at the moment. Maybe you wouldn't mind coming in a little later, to the office, I mean, and someone can take your statement, then."

"This is hard to believe. My God, I'm telling you that the man who killed my brother was here. Not more than ten or fifteen minutes ago."

"Did he *say* that to you, Miss Nichols? That he killed your brother?"

"Of course not."

"And have you seen this man before?"

"No. I don't think so. But I *have* heard him before. On the telephone."

"Would you like me to notify Kennedy Whelan about all of this, Miss Nichols?"

"Of course I would."

"Do you want to speak to him personally? I can have him come over there, even though your brother's case is closed—officially, I mean."

"If you think it's necessary. Yes."

"Good. I'll see to it as soon as possible." A brief pause, then, "Miss Nichols?"

"Yes?"

"You said this man, this hunter, left not more than ten or fifteen minutes ago. If it's so urgent—

and I'm not saying it isn't—why did you wait so long before calling? I'm just curious."

She thought a moment, then said, "I don't know. 'Ten or fifteen minutes' is just a figure of speech, isn't it? It could just have easily been only a couple of minutes."

"Yes, I suppose that's true, Miss Nichols. At any rate, I'll call Mr. Whelan as soon as possible and I'm sure he'll get back to you. Thanks very much for calling."

"Wait a minute."

"Yes?"

"Don't you even want a description of this man?"

"Oh. Yes, I do. Of course. Let me find a pen." A brief pause. "Okay, go ahead."

Katherine described the man, and then Busher said, "Thank you again, Miss Nichols. I'm sure Mr. Whelan will be very interested in this." And he hung up.

Katherine didn't hang up. She stared incredulously at the phone for several moments. "My God," she whispered, then put the receiver down, crossed the kitchen to the back door, and pushed it open. She heard from here and there in the bright sunlit grasses:

"Are you getting tired? Do you want some tea?"

268

"Do you want tea?"

"I have tea."

She took a step down, so she was closer to the voices.

They continued:

"And a drowsy numbness pains my sense . . .
As though of hemlock I had drunk. . . ."

"I know what thirst is."

"It's for the taste. For the body. For the tongue and the stomach. It relieves. Or it needs relief. It comes and goes. You pour water on it. So you pour tea on it. It goes away. The thirst. The fire. The heat of the day, the heat of the evening, and the conflagration."

"Do you want some tea? Some lemonade? I have gallons of lemonade, sticky and pink."

"I weep for Adonais—he is dead!
Oh, weep for Adonais! though our tears
Thaw not the frost which binds so dear a
     head!"

She continued down the steps, her gait slow. She listened. She heard, "I know what thirst is."

"It's for the taste."

*"And a drowsy numbness pains my sense . . .
As though of hemlock I had drunk."*

"That's Keats."

"Poor dead cold Keats."

She saw movement in the quack grass. She stopped walking. She pleaded, "Who *are* you?"

And she heard, "We are here for you. We offer much comfort."

"Good comfort."

"Good tea."

"And comfort."

"But not much in the way of warmth, I'm afraid, which we had then, but do not have now, and never again will, though we have . . ."

". . . its close approximation in fire."

"Again and again and again and again."

She backed away from the movement, and the voices, up the steps, into her house.

Chapter Thirty-six

Eight days after the murder of Tim Lowe

"Hi," Kennedy Whelan said to Bill Straub, who had answered the door. "Remember me?"

"Sure," Bill answered.

"Can we talk?"

"About that guy I found?" Bill gave Whelan an intense, expectant grin. "Did you find out what killed him?"

"We think so. Your name's Bill, isn't it?"

"Bill Straub, yes, sir. What killed him, then?"

"In all probability, it was what we call 'natural causes.' Can I come in?"

Bill opened the door wide. "Sure. My dad's not here, though. He's out showing a house. He's a real estate man, you know."

"Yes, I know."

"And he's showing a house." Bill closed the

door. "What does 'natural causes' mean, anyway? Does it mean like a spider bite or something?"

"Not exactly," Whelan answered. He nodded toward the cluttered living room. "Do you mind if I sit down?"

Bill shook his head. "I don't mind. Go ahead and sit down."

Whelan went into the living room and sat in an armless ladder-back chair. He looked very uncomfortable, but the rest of the furniture was apparently used as a dumping ground for old newspapers and magazines. Whelan said, "Do you want to answers some questions for me, Bill?"

Bill grinned again. "You think he was murdered, huh?" He grabbed another ladder-back chair from near the entrance to the living room, put it in front of Whelan's chair, and sat backward on it, so his chin rested on top of it. "I thought so, too."

Whelan smiled. "No one's mentioned the word *murder*, Bill. We're just looking into every possibility."

"He was pretty young, that guy, wasn't he?"

"Yes, he was. In his late twenties."

"Yeah, that's pretty young. What was it then, these natural causes? Was it like a heart attack?"

"It's a possibility."

"Yeah, pretty young, like I said. Just like Mrs. Gore."

"Who's that?"

"She used to live in that house there, Katherine's house . . ."

"You call her by her first name, Bill?"

"Sure, she said I could." He was whining a little.

"Oh? You talk to her quite a lot?"

"Sometimes." He was getting tense.

"You like talking to her?"

"Sure I do. I guess anybody would."

"Oh?" Whelan put on a look of confusion. "Why would you say that?"

Bill shrugged. "I don't know. She's pretty hot, don't you think?"

"You've slept with her, have you, Bill?"

Bill's mouth dropped open. He shook his head quickly.

"Bill," Whelan continued, "it's not against the law to sleep with someone."

"I didn't . . . I mean, *we* didn't—"

"Tell me about that morning again, Bill. About finding the body—"

"I mean," Bill cut in, "I thought about it. I thought about it. Shit, anybody would."

"Not anybody, Bill. Now please tell me about finding the body."

"Wouldn't you?"

"Wouldn't I what?"

"Think about, you know, about what you said—"

"That's neither here nor there, Bill."

"But I didn't *do* anything. I wouldn't ever *do* anything." He was very tense, now.

"But she wanted you to, didn't she, Bill?"

"Huh?"

"Because I saw the way she was dressed that morning, and if ever I've seen an invitation before—"

"She told me to get away from her!" Bill interrupted; there was anger in his voice. "All I did was put my hands on her shoulders and she told me to get away from her! Jeez—I didn't mean nothin' by it—"

Whelan stood. "That's all, Bill." He started for the door.

Bill called after him, "Hey, I didn't answer your question."

Whelan said nothing. He was fighting the anger building inside him. "Goddamned fool!" he was saying to himself. The intensity of his anger surprised him. He didn't like making mistakes, and he liked even less having to admit them to

274

himself. He knew that at that moment he could easily kill someone, and the knowledge was not only frightening, it was uplifting.

The man's given name was Chester Lee Manning. He had always liked his name. He thought it was "dignified," and woe to anyone, even a friend, who tried to call him "Chester Lee." It was Chester, or it was "Mr. Manning."

He was just over six feet tall, with a big, square head, close-set, rheumy blue eyes, and grayish yellow skin. And he had been hunting the woods around the township of Willow Point for nearly forty of his fifty-one years. He'd killed more than sixty deer, a hundred raccoons, a thousand squirrels, several dozen opossums, and one man. Jason Nichols.

It had happened with incredible swiftness. Chester had heard movement in the underbrush nearby and he turned, leveled his rifle, grinned— as he always did just before a kill—and then had seen Jason's face. He saw surprise in it, and a little fear, but he saw thankfulness, too, because clearly Chester had seen him—Jason—in the nick of time.

But in that instant, something inside Chester's head flip-flopped. *Hell,* he thought, though not in so many words, *I've killed raccoons and opos-*

sums and deer, but I've never killed a man! It
was a very powerful impulse, and he gave it free
rein just long enough—a millisecond—that his
finger half closed, half twitched on the trigger in
response. *It's like a game!* his brain screamed at
him. And the rifle discharged. Jason's face ceased
to exist.

Chester stayed very still for several minutes,
the rifle leveled on the spot where Jason's face
had been. He was trying hard to decide how he
felt about what he'd just done. He knew that in
the instant the rifle had discharged, he had been
enjoying himself immensely. It was a sexual enjoyment, he knew—the exercise of power. But,
as the seconds passed, his enjoyment was replaced by an overwhelming fear. More than a few
of his friends knew what he was doing today, and
although most of them could be counted on to
keep their mouths shut, there was Loomis, who
might not, and Schneider, who for sure
wouldn't. And Chester didn't relish the idea of a
few years in prison—better to exit life the way
this poor slob just had. In an instant.

So, he had planted Jason's body in Katherine's
garden. He congratulated himself on the idea.
She'd be blamed, of course. She was new to the
area, a little strange . . .

It was not until several days later that he

learned his victim had been Katherine's brother, and that made him very happy. Everyone knew that most murders were family affairs.

Chester said to himself now, eight weeks later, "You got big brass balls, Chester." Because he was hunting the area near Katherine's property again. He liked shooting does especially; he wasn't sure why. He remembered that once, years before, a woman had seen a doe slung across the hood of his car and she'd hollered at him, "Bambi killer!" And he remembered grinning hard at her and shouting back, "Fuck yes, oh, fuck yes!" which had surprised him, because it had been so spontaneous. He enjoyed his spontaneity. It made life more interesting not knowing what his brain and body were going to do from one moment to the next. Sometimes it got him into trouble, sure—like with Jason Nichols—but he was smart enough, wasn't he, and he could work it out. He'd proved that.

He could see Katherine's house from where he stood, just inside the stand of woods. It was a bright, brisk morning, and visibility was perfect— the gently rolling fields that spread out in front of him had the crisp, clear look of a very good photograph.

He was thinking about going to Katherine's house again. He didn't know what he'd do when he got there—that was for *when* he got there, for when she opened the door and heard his voice again and maybe, this time, made the connection to the voice she'd heard on the phone a week after her brother's death. He didn't know what he'd do if she did make that connection. He told himself that he couldn't even guess.

He whispered, "Expectation's everything, Chester!" Then he stopped thinking about Katherine because images were crowding into his head and betraying to him what he was probably going to do her. He didn't want to know what he was going to do. Knowing took the fun away.

He kept his gaze on the rutted earth in front of him and moved carefully over it. Now and then he glanced up, toward the house, and the images of Katherine crowded back, and he pushed them away.

He looked up at one point and saw something dark and quick moving in front of the tall quack grass just ahead. He lifted his head and looked into the tight, clear blue sky, because low-flying hawks often cast shadows that were similar to what he'd just seen. The sky was empty. He lowered his head. He forgot what he'd seen.

Chester Lee Manning had always hunted alone. He got along well with practically no one because he was argumentative, unpredictable, and just bright enough to feel certain that he was smarter than any of those who knew him.

He was a loner, and he was also lonely, though he wouldn't have admitted it. He knew there was something missing inside him, and there were even rare times that he ached a little because of it.

But no one ever asked Hayward Sloat much about himself—beyond the formalities of everyday life, his name, his age (thirty-six on the night of the fire that destroyed Orchid Street), and his occupation (caretaker). He lived alone inside his little house on Orchid Street. And an entity that he knew nothing about lived inside him. It forced him from his bed in the morning, and into the bathroom, to the breakfast table, to work, and home again.

And, on certain nights, it forced him from the house and onto the street, then into the shadows, where it reached from deep inside him, and moved him, as if he were a marionette, and made him do the things he could not help doing—the things he knew he really did not want to do, but which felt very, very good to do.

Chester Lee Manning told himself again, *Hawks make that kind of shadow.* And he looked into the tight blue sky and saw, again, that it was empty. He stopped walking. "Hello?"

he said. Ahead of him, the tall quack grass was very still and very bright. Beyond it, something moved slowly and gracefully, something that was dark and hunched over slightly, as if trying—somehow playfully—to hide itself.

Chester heard then, from far to his right,

*"Art thou pale for weariness
Of climbing heaven and gazing on the
    earth . . ."*

Chester looked toward the source of the voice. The voice continued:

*"And ever changing, like a joyless eye—
"Tell me, thou Star, whose wings of life
Speed thee in thy fiery flight."*

Chester growled at the voice, "What the fuck are you sayin', boy?" though he could see no one.

Then, out of the corner of his eye, he saw that the dark form ahead of him was moving, and he snapped his gaze toward it. Dimly, he heard these words from far to his right, *"In what cavern of the night/Will thy pinions close now?"* The words were spoken very quickly, as if in a panic.

Chester saw a half dozen people gathered

loosely nearby, all looking at him calmly, several smiling, as if in pleasure.

Slowly, they backed off into the bright quack grass.

And life began to ease out of him.

He saw this: houses rising up around him out of the quack grass; he smelled garbage, freshly washed laundry, gasoline . . . cloves . . .

Larry Cage, coming down from the bedroom to the kitchen, thought it was about time he was honest with himself, about time he admitted that his relationship with Katherine was going flat and that he didn't much care. Hell, the things she wanted out of life weren't the things he wanted. Of course, Lord knew what she wanted lately, except to paint, and even that seemed to be slipping away from her.

Hell yes—he told himself—he still loved her. Why not? Love wasn't something that just evaporated over a couple of weeks. Or at least it wasn't supposed to.

He'd grown . . . beyond her. He'd outgrown her. She was living in some kind of fantasy world. Sure. This house, and the land around it. The need to get away and be a hermit. It was a pleasant fantasy, but it wasn't very realistic, was it?

He'd stick around for a while, anyway. Why not? She was fun. She was good in the sack.

Of course, it would have been nice if she'd learned to cook, and it would have been nice if she'd found better uses for the money her father had left her.

Katherine came in from the back porch, then, painting supplies in both hands. She nodded at Larry and said, "Hi. I think I'm going to take a little walk before I get going on this today."

"Oh?" He poured himself a cup of coffee, put a teaspoon of sugar in it. "Where to?"

She smiled oddly. "A friend's house." She set her painting supplies on the kitchen table.

"A friend? I didn't know you had any friends out here." He brought his cup of coffee to the table, sat down with it. "It's nice that you do."

Katherine nodded. "Her name's Gloria. She was here once."

"She lives nearby?"

"I'm not sure." She shook her head. "That sounds stupid, doesn't it? What I mean is, I'm not really sure *where* her house is. I know it's somewhere behind those woods." She nodded toward them. "And I'd like to go looking for it. She's good to talk to."

"And I'm not?" Larry asked.

She studied his face for a moment, then said,

"Where'd that question come from?"

He shook his head. "Nowhere. Forget it. I was just thinking that when you come back . . . I was thinking . . . about us." He hesitated. "That sounds pretty ominous, doesn't it?"

"Later," she told him, unconcerned. "We'll talk later, okay?"

"Okay," he said.

Late morning

Kennedy Whelan said to Larry Cage, who had answered the knock at Katherine's door, "Who are you?"

Larry answered, "I live here. Who are you?"

Whelan produced his shield. "I'm Kennedy Whelan. I'm looking into the murder of Jason Nichols. Is Katherine at home?"

"I had assumed that case was closed, Mr. Whelan. No, she's not at home. Did you come to get your money? I'll take care of it. Is a check okay?"

"Money? What money?"

"You left Katherine a bill for damages to your suit—"

"Oh," Whelan cut in. "No. That's not important. Forget it. Where'd she go?"

"I don't know. A walk. She said she was going to a friend's house. I'll have her give you a call when she gets back."

283

"A friend's house? What friend?"

Larry shrugged. "Someone named Gloria."

"Do you mind if I wait?"

Larry opened the door wide. "Okay. If you need to."

Whelan hesitated. "On second thought, maybe I'll go looking for her. Where does her friend live?"

Larry smiled uneasily. "It sounds pretty urgent."

"It isn't. I just need to ask her some questions. So her friend lives where?"

"I don't know, I'm not sure . . ."

"Which direction did she take, Mr. Cage? Did she go up the road"—he nodded to his left—"that way . . ."

"No. She went out back. Through the fields."

"How long ago?"

"Fifteen minutes, I guess."

Whelan nodded toward the inside of the house. "Can I go through here?"

"Yeah, sure." Larry stepped out of the way. "Be my guest."

Whelan stepped past him. "Thank you," Whelan said, and moved through the living room at a stiff, fast walk.

Larry called after him, "Hey, do you mind if I join you?"

But Whelan was through the living room already, and into the kitchen, and did not hear him.

Larry went to the back door, pushed it open, stood with his hand holding it. He watched as Whelan jogged through the backyard and into the tall quack grass beyond. "It's pretty treacherous out there," he called. Whelan lifted his arm a little in acknowledgment.

Chapter Thirty-seven

Katherine peered in through the long, rectangular windows in the front door of the huge house; as she had weeks earlier, she saw the vague suggestion of a kitchen at the end of a long hallway.

"Gloria?" she called.

She thought the house had an empty feel, an aura of abandonment. And a faint but unmistakable odor, too. The odor of wood smoke.

"Gloria," she called again, and added, "Are you in there?"

She heard a stiff rustling sound in the quack grass behind her, as if someone was walking in it. She turned, looked. She saw the form of a man standing in the grass a dozen feet away. "Hello," she called, and the form stepped forward and appeared to nod to indicate the house.

Katherine said, "Who are you?"

And she heard a man's voice say, "These are *things*, and they are easy to believe in. Houses and shoes, for instance. Horses and goats. Hooves of hoofed animals. Ketchup bottles and little restaurants and men in bow ties. Trees as well, and the fires that destroy them, the fires that destroy us all. But heaven is harder and love is harder still and memories do not always stick, but there is rain and the sound of rain and the noises of children, and the children, too . . ."

"I don't understand you," Katherine said. "I'm looking for Gloria—"

"If you come upon a burning street," said the dark form of the man, "run and hide and listen, because the fire is always advancing, always approaching, always ready."

Katherine heard a woman's voice, then, from farther away. "Who's Gloria?" it said.

"Great big fat woman," the man's voice said.

"Lives down the street in a big fat house," said yet another voice.

Katherine said uneasily, "Do you know where she is? I'm looking for her. I want to talk to her— I need to talk to her."

"Can't," said the man.

"Can't," said the woman.

"You don't understand," Katherine pleaded. "She's my friend."

"We all are," said the man.

"We all are," said the woman.

"Except," said another voice, "for Mr. Sloat. Believe in him. He's a thing to encounter."

"Yes," said the man's voice, "he's always skulking about—"

"Always skulking about," said the woman.

"Loving people into the hereafter, poor miserable thing."

"It's out of affection that he does it. Such an affectionate and miserable thing."

"Who are you?" Katherine said.

"Who are we?"

"She wants to know who we are."

"Who are we?"

"We're things beyond even our own dreams. . . ."

"But who in this place can dream? Or dreams? Or sleeps? Or even gets up to pee?"

". . . and we're having trouble, that's what we are."

". . . . with eternity. We can't get hold of it. Who can? Only the miserable try."

"And who's Gloria?" said a voice.

"Great big fat woman—"

"Lives down the street."

"In a house big enough for her, a house big as Cincinnati."

"Prances about in it naked day and night. Putting on a show. The neighbors are mortified."

"The neighbors are dead and mortified."

"The neighbors are cold, dead, and mortified and all fired up."

"Please," said Katherine, "if you *know* where I can find Gloria . . ."

"You know where she is, my dear."

"Katherine?" It was Whelan's voice.

Katherine glanced at Gloria's house, behind her, in the direction of Whelan's voice. The house looked grainy, like a photograph made with substandard film.

"Katherine?" she heard again, closer.

She looked back, toward the spot where the man had been, and the woman. She saw only quack grass. She looked at the house again. "Katherine?" she heard. "Answer me." The house was gone. "Don't give me any trouble, Katherine." Then Whelan appeared, ten feet away. "Hello," he said. "Do you mind if we go back to your place and talk?"

Katherine ran.

Whelan cursed and put his hand inside his jacket, on his holstered .38. "Please stop!" he shouted.

Katherine continued running.

"Don't make this hard on both of us," Whelan shouted. "All I want to do is talk."

His voice grew fainter as Katherine ran from him. She stumbled, nearly fell, pushed herself up, her open hands sinking several inches into the soft earth.

I've got her now! Whelan thought. *I've got her. She's mine.* He was glad she'd run from him. He had hoped she would. He went after her at a quick walk. He had no reason to run—she'd tire quickly. "Katherine," he called, "just a few quick questions." He smiled. This was working out quite nicely.

He thought he saw her just ahead, partially hidden by tall grasses. His mind replayed for him what he'd seen of her moments earlier, when he had come upon her. She was wearing jeans, he remembered, a light-colored blouse. And what he saw just ahead, shimmering a little, was very dark, and tall. Whelan's hand closed on his .38. He stopped walking. "Who's there?" he said. He got no answer. "Who's there?" he repeated, louder. "I'm a police officer. I have a gun!"

The dark form just ahead moved to its left, as if trying to hide behind taller grasses there.

Whelan found that was he was trembling, and it angered him. He pulled his .38 out, leveled it

291

at the form just ahead. "Step out of there, now!" he ordered.

But the form was gone before he'd finished his sentence.

Katherine was waiting for him on her back porch steps. She was sitting on the top step, with her elbows on her knees and her hands clasped. She looked very casual.

Whelan approached her slowly and deliberately across the backyard, much as Chester Lee Manning had, and when he opened his mouth to speak, she said, "I'm sorry I ran. You startled me."

"So am I, Katherine," he said, but his timing was off and his attempt at a brusque *I'm in command here!* tone unconvincing.

"You said you wanted to talk," she told him. "Did Mr. Busher call you?"

Whelan stopped at the bottom of the steps; it occurred to him that he'd tried this tactic before, a week ago, and it hadn't worked then. "No," he said. "Did he have a reason to call me?"

"I think so," Katherine said.

Whelan said, "I don't like you." He took a quick, deep breath; the remark had been sudden and spontaneous, and he knew that if he'd thought first, he wouldn't have said it. But he realized there was no calling it back, now, and that to apologize for it or to try and put it behind him by ignoring it would be a mistake. He patted his suit for a cigar, found one in his inside coat pocket, took it out, lit it. He realized that she'd been smiling coyly at him for the last few seconds. He told her, "You're not getting away with anything, Katherine."

She said, "And you're not going to believe this, but I'm not really *trying* to." She stood, turned, crossed the porch to the back door, glanced around, "Will that be all, Mr. Whelan?"

"No," he managed, surprised by her casual tone.

"Oh?" Out of the corner of her eye she could see that Larry was standing just inside the door, as if hiding.

"I wanted to talk to you about Bill Straub."

"I think not, Mr. Whelan."

He stepped forward, so he was at the bottom of the back steps. "You think not?" He smiled. She watched him take a long drag on the cigar, watching him exhale, watched the smoke dissipate on a sudden breeze. "Does your *boyfriend* know about Bill Straub, Katherine?" It was worth a try.

She saw Larry step back from the door. She came to the top of the steps, anger pushing through her. "Do you have a warrant of some kind, Mr. Whelan?" Her voice was quivering.

"A warrant, Katherine?"

"Yes. Are you going to arrest me?"

"No. Not at this time."

"Then what in the *hell* are you doing here?"

He took the cigar from his mouth, let it fall to the ground, crushed it with the toe of his shoe. "Just asking questions."

"No. That's not what you're doing!" She pointed stiffly at the cigar. "And pick that disgusting thing up!"

He glanced at it, then at her, shrugged. "Sure." He bent over, picked it up, and shoved it into his pants pocket. "Anything you say, Katherine." He was rattling her, he realized.

"Don't call me by my first name. I never gave you permission to do that."

"I know it. I just thought that we'd become . . . close."

"You bastard!"

He grinned. He liked rattling her. "So tell me— *does* your boyfriend know about the Straub kid?"

"Does he know *what,* for Christ's sake?"

"That you've been sleeping with him."

Katherine had been expecting the question,

294

but it took her a moment to respond. "Is that what Bill told you?"

"Not in so many words."

"Goddamn you, answer my question! Did Bill say that he and I had been sleeping together?" She was nearly shouting now and was well aware that Larry could hear her.

Whelan answered, "No. That's not what he told me. Not in so many words. He didn't need to say it in so many words."

"Get off my property!"

He had expected that. "Of course," he said, and started walking slowly around the east side of the house.

"And the next time—" Katherine began, but Whelan interrupted.

"I know, the next time I'd better have a warrant." He grinned again. "I will." He quickened his pace; moments later, he had disappeared around the side of the house.

"You handled him well," Larry said. He was standing near the back door as Katherine came in. "I listened," he went on, and repeated, "You handled him well."

She glanced at him. "How'd he know where I was, Larry?"

"Sorry."

"How did that asshole know where the fuck I was? Is it such a hard question to answer? Did *you* tell him?"

Larry smiled nervously. "Sure. Why not? He just wanted to ask you some questions. It's best not to fool with people like him. Especially him. He's got a chip on his shoulder the size of Jupiter."

"I wish you hadn't told him where I was, Larry. I really wish you hadn't told him where I was."

"Yeah, I know. But he's very . . . He seems to have a lot of . . . I'm sorry, but I think I was simply reacting to the fact that he was a cop. Anyone else would have reacted the same damned way, Katherine." He smiled again and nodded toward the stove. "I made some coffee. Do you want some?"

"No."

He went over to the stove. She could see that he was nervous and she found it annoying.

He said as he poured his coffee, "Who's this Bill Straub character he was talking about?" He glanced at her and smiled as if to say he was merely curious.

"He's just one of the local kids, Larry. He's on the high school track team, I guess, and he runs through here, through the property. I've told you about him."

Larry brought his cup over to the table and set it down. He continued standing. He grinned crookedly. "And *have* you been sleeping with him?"

She started to leave the room. "I'll forget you asked me that question, Larry."

"I'm curious," he said. "Really. Just curious." He caught her by the arm, held it tight.

She glanced confusedly at his hand. "Let go, Larry."

"I want to know." He was still smiling. He wanted very much to let go of her arm, as she'd asked, and to stop smiling, but he couldn't. He said, "I just want to know. I want to know the truth."

She repeated, in the same tone of smoldering tension that she'd just used, "Let go of me, Larry!"

He squeezed harder, despite himself. "You didn't, didn't you? What is he? Fifteen, sixteen?"

"Let go of me, Larry!"

His smile broadened. "I'm sorry." He thought he sounded sincere, but he continued holding her arm tightly. "I'm sorry. I'm not accusing you. I understand. Really, I do understand."

"Please let go of me!"

"I understand more than you know, Katherine. I'm not an idiot." He felt her arm stiffen. "I'm not blind, and I'm not deaf—"

"I'll hurt you, Larry!"

"Sure," he said. "I know." He felt his smile flicker off for a moment, and he tried to keep it off, but it returned, bigger and sillier than before, because he was very nervous and it was all but paralyzing him. "I know you want to hurt me. But tell me, please—and not just about the Straub boy—but about your brother, too. Please, I want to know, I *need*—"

A year earlier, after a skiing accident, Larry had been bedridden for a month with three broken ribs. One of the ribs hadn't healed properly and it was into this rib that Katherine now pushed her free elbow very hard. He let go of her at once and then, for several seconds, stood with his mouth open and his hand moving with incredible slowness to his rib cage. His eyes were wide. He wasn't breathing. Then, as Katherine watched, and tried to decide what to do (leave the room, apologize, wait), she heard sharp, puppylike squeaks of pain come from him.

"Larry, I'm sorry," she began, and stopped. She realized it was a stupid thing to say because it was untrue.

The squeaks continued. His hand found his rib

cage at last, and his head lowered, again with incredible slowness. A look of great, pained disbelief came over him. He knees buckled. And then he was down on all fours beside the table. His squeaks became low, short-lived moans that were in time with his breathing, which was agony.

Katherine stared at him for a few moments. Then she turned sharply and left the room.

Chapter Thirty-eight

He emptied his closet and took his pillow and packed his bags. He decided he'd sleep in the living room that night. He had forgotten to take a blanket off the bed, and because he didn't feel like confronting Katherine again—she was in the bedroom, now—he covered himself with a sports jacket he rarely wore. He was angry but thought he'd get over it. And he was feeling sorry for himself, too, but he knew he'd get over that. And he was experiencing lots of pain, which he tried futilely to ignore. Every once in a while he raised his head a little from the couch, looked toward the upstairs bedroom, and whispered, "Fucking bitch!" It gave him momentary comfort.

He was watched as he waited for sleep. At several windows, faces looked in—nearly completed faces, with eyes that could almost see and mouths that could almost move and laugh.

Behind the windows, in the brisk, clear September night, the faces looked as if they could have been masks, because they were still and quiet. Something that once was curiosity existed behind them. Now it was more akin to the pull of strings and the tug of wires. Now it could cause a head to tilt, a smile to start. It was the sad and futile approximation of life, nothing more.

Larry rolled over on the couch so he was facing the back of it, so his weight was off his rib. He whispered into the couch, "Fucking bitch!" and a small fantasy started. It had to do with salving his ego, which had been so badly bruised, with showing his strength, after all. It was a timid fantasy and he felt ashamed for it, but he watched, anyway, as it grew, halted, shrank, then grew again and swaggered about. He knew that he'd shoo it away after a while, when he was done with it.

At one of the windows, a face frowned. A downward tug of the lips. They were good lips, a woman's lips, on an exquisite Mediterranean face. The frown became fixed and unmoving; the eyes, which were large and brown and erotic—though, oddly, even more erotic now than when life was in them—leveled on the man trying to sleep, and saw into him. The frown altered, the eyes altered, because the thing behind them that had once been a brain was remembering another man, in another time, whose thoughts had been violent, too. And something that once had been hate and grief welled up inside the woman. And she passed with consummate grace through the window and into the room.

The jacket that Larry Cage had covered himself with was made of wool and where it touched his bare arms it itched. He scratched distractedly and unrolled the sleeves of his long-sleeved shirt. He heard these words from his own mouth, "Who's there? Katherine?" His brow furrowed. He wanted to know why he'd said it, because it had surprised him. He whispered again, "Fucking bitch!" It was an attempt to calm his sudden anxiety; he told himself that he hadn't lived in the house long enough to become accustomed to the night's pitch-darkness. He pulled his sports jacket up until it covered his bare neck, rolled to his back, and opened his eyes so they were looking at the ceiling. His peripheral vision showed him something pale and oblong nearby, and a small grunt of confusion escaped him. He rolled to his side again, faced the couch. He said very softly into it, "Katherine?" And heard in response a high-pitched, ragged humming sound.

. . . the body of Christina Marchetti sat up suddenly in the tall weeds where it had been put. This was no great feat—corpses had been known to sit up from time to time. But then, with the sunlight on her, she turned her head and her closed eyes in the direction of her house and her children, and a grief so intense that it penetrated death itself tore through her. And her vocal cords—in the initial stages of decomposition . . .

Christina Marchetti screamed again, in the dark, cold room where Larry Cage waited for sleep, and Larry Cage stiffened up so his fists clenched and his fingernails drew blood from his palms and his knees pulled up to his chin and he found himself screaming, too, in an attempt to the block the awful scream of the thing standing in the room with him.

Katherine heard it. It was a continuous, high-pitched, and brittle noise, like a scream that is done from the deep recesses of pain and memory.

She listened for a long while, until at last the scream stopped. Then her eyes opened. She became aware that she was not alone in the room. "Larry," she said, "was that you?" though she knew well enough that it wasn't. She heard then, very faintly, as if she were hearing it through several layers of thick clothing, "Lazarus is scared of the dark."

"Who's Lazarus?" she said, and found that she was smiling. She got no answer. Another voice, closer, from the corner of the room, said, "You're getting too old for that, boy." It was a woman's voice, strong, harsh, and scolding. It repeated itself once, then again, and again.

Katherine asked, still smiling, "Who's Lazarus?"

A voice said, "She wants to know who Lazarus is, for Christ's sake."

"Who does?" said a man's voice.

"Her," a woman's voice answered. "There in the bed."

"In the bed?"

"In the bed there."

And Katherine said, "Who's in the room, please? Gloria, is that you?"

"She wants to know if Gloria's here."

"Gloria? Who's that?"

"Great big fat woman, lives in a big fat house."

"I ain't seen her."

Katherine swung her feet to the floor. The bare wood was cold and she lifted her feet at once. "Who's there, please?" she said, and realized that she was pleading. She put her feet on the floor again and held them there, as if through force of will. She said again, at a whisper, "Who's there, please?"

The voices stopped, except for one, the voice of a child, which said, *"Mia madre,"* on a descending note, and repeated it, *"Mia madre . . ."*

Katherine stood. She was naked and the idea came to her that Jason was going to rush into the room—*Putting on a show for the townies, sis?* It was something he had done quite often. Poor man. He had a problem.

She sneezed. The cold floor, she thought. It was giving her a virus.

Her warm, terry cloth robe was at the foot of the bed. She picked it up and shrugged into it.

Larry Cage was dawdling. Asking questions he really shouldn't ask. Getting in the way of her peace and quiet.

She sneezed again, looked around for her slippers, saw them just under the bed, toed them out, put them on.

Peace and quiet! It was why she had moved to this house, after all. To get away from the bullies who wanted to push her around. Like Kennedy Whelan. And Larry. And even Jason. A lot of bullies. A lot of pushing around.

But not Gloria. Gloria didn't push her around. She couldn't. Gloria was dead. And Gloria cared for her.

Katherine went to the window. She saw darkness, little else. Only shapes, suggestions of movement. She smelled gasoline, and garbage, too, tomato sauce. And cloves. It was an odd mixture of smells and she inhaled deeply to capture and hold it. She smiled and felt comforted.

Then she moved away from the window and went to the door, opened it, stepped into the hallway. Below, she could hear that Larry was whimpering. She liked that. *Hang on tight, Larry!* She went to the stairway, then down to the living room, where Larry lay on his side on the couch, with his fists clenched near his mouth.

Katherine said nothing to him. She realized that she had had nothing to say to him for quite a while, for months. Let him whimper. He deserved to whimper.

The she turned from him, scraped her ankle against the leg of her white wicker chair, noted the sudden, short-lived pain, grimaced.

Peace and quiet. She deserved that, didn't she? And if she had to go to Gloria for it, if that was the only place she could find it, then that was the way it had to be.

She rubbed the ankle, although the pain was gone. She rubbed it because she was remembering the pain and wanted it back, because she knew where she was going, now. Because she knew there would be no such mundane pain as that, ever again—just the hollow pain of looking back and knowing the bitter taste of things that had gone by. But peace and quiet, too. And no more bullying.

She stopped rubbing her ankle. She went into the kitchen, through it, to the back door. She pushed the door open and stepped out into the night.

Chapter Thirty-nine

Kennedy Whelan shoved his hands into his pants pocket, found a thick residue of tobacco, and grimaced. "Mr. Cage?" he called. "Miss Nichols?" He was growing impatient. He'd been standing at the front door for several minutes and the chill morning air was beginning to bother him.

He knocked on the door again, very loudly, waited a moment, then went to the front window, put his face to it, and peered in. He saw no one. He went back to the door, tried the knob. The door was unlocked. He pushed it open, stuck his head in, called, "Hello?" then glanced around at Katherine's Toyota and Larry Cage's Ford in the driveway. He looked into the house again. "Hello?" he repeated, then stepped in.

He went to the living room first. It was empty.

Then he followed the short hallway to the kitchen. He found Larry Cage seated at the small kitchen table. He had his arms crossed in front of him and he was dressed in blue pajamas and a wool sports jacket. He had a two-day growth of beard and his eyes were nearly puffed shut by what Whelan thought looked like exhaustion.

It was midmorning, but the kitchen was poorly lighted, so he flicked on the overhead light. When he had a good view of Larry Cage, he exclaimed, "Good Christ, man!"

Larry's head moved very slowly, as if Whelan had taken him by surprise but he didn't have the strength to react quickly. He looked at Whelan a moment, a little openmouthed, and said, "Oh, it's you." A short pause. "Katherine isn't here." And he turned his head back. "I don't know where she is."

"Her car's here," Whelan said.

Larry said nothing.

Whelan went on, "Did she go out? For a walk?"

Larry shook his head. "No, I don't believe she did."

"Do you know *where* she went?"

A small, quivering, clearly self-pitying smile flickered across Larry's face. "I don't know if *she*

310

could tell you that, Mr. Whelan."

"Well then, how long ago did she leave?"

"She left a couple of days ago. I'm waiting for her."

"You're waiting for her?"

"Yes. To come back."

"And when will that be?"

"I don't know. She didn't say."

"I mean"—Whelan was growing impatient—"will it be this morning, this afternoon?"

"Sure. Any time. It could be any time. Tomorrow. I don't know."

Whelan stepped forward, shoved his hands into his pockets, and began fingering the mess of tobacco there. "Why are you giving me a hard time, Mr. Cage? I only wanted to talk to her. I wanted to tell her that we're letting her off the hook. I wanted her to know that we've got a suspect."

"Oh?"

"We've got a name, anyway. A local man. We're looking for him, now." A short pause. "Are you all right, Mr. Cage?"

"I don't know," Larry answered. "I don't think so. I don't think that I'm at all all right." He pushed his chair away from the table with effort, then stood shakily. "I haven't eaten in a while."

T. M. WRIGHT

He turned, using the back of the chair for support. The kitchen was cool and damp, and he gathered his sports jacket around himself, then went to the back door and stood unsteadily at it, with his back to Whelan.

A long silence followed. At last, Whelan stopped fingering the tobacco in his pants pockets. "Could you tell her that for me, please?" he said.

"Yes," Larry answered.

"About this local man, I mean.

"I know what you meant," Larry said. His back was still turned. "I'll tell her."

"Thanks," Whelan said. "And would you tell her please that I'm sorry if I hassled her unduly? It was nothing personal."

Larry grinned a little. "Aren't we all sorry, Mr. Whelan?" he said, then added, "Good-bye."

Whelan said nothing. He turned, passed through the hallway, and out of the house.

In the fields behind the house

"Does he have a name?"

"He takes care of everything."

"He had a name, once. When he was killing us."

312

"Does *who* have a name?"

"Him. There. Him skulking around. He's always skulking around. He thinks it's part of the act."

"The act?"

"Of course he has a name. Everyone does. Who's without a name? What a consequence."

"My dear, do you miss him?"

"Is this an act?"

"No, I don't think I do."

"My heart aches . . ."

"Who's that?"

". . . and a drowsy numbness pains my sense as if of hemlock I had drunk."

"That's Keats."

"Cold Keats."

"Poor dead cold Keats."

"No, Gloria, I don't think that I miss him."

"Gloria? Who's Gloria?"

"Great big fat woman, lives down the street."

"Down the street? What street?"

"This street."

"What street is that?"

"It's not very warm here, though. It's not what I expected."

"I don't know. I did know, once."

"It never is, my dear."

"It's Orchid Street."

"Short, cold street."

"Orchid Street. We had a fire here, once. Bad fire."

"Poor dead cold street."

"Hot street, once. Very hot. Very steamy."

"Much have I traveled in the realms of gold
And many goodly states and kingdoms seen.
Round many western islands have I been
Which bards in fealty to Apollo hold."

"He's off again."

"Who is?"

"Him there. Poor Gabriel. Poor cold Gabriel."

"Some lemonade, my dear? It comes to me
that I drank lots of lemonade."

"Lemonade? she said. Lemonade?"

"What's lemonade?"

"It's for the mouth. For taste. For thirst."

"I miss Jason, though. I loved Jason. Is he
here?"

"I know what thirst is."

"Mia madre!"

"That man who skulks about is kind of a caretaker."

"He takes care . . ."

314

"... of us ..."

"No, I'm sorry, but Jason's not here."

"Who?"

"Him there. Him. Skulking about. He's always skulking about."

Larry left the kitchen and went to the stairs, up to Katherine's bedroom. He hoped to see her there. He thought he had seen her earlier. He wasn't sure.

"I remember now. It was iced tea. Gallons of iced tea. Whole gallons of iced tea. All day. Every day. All summer long. Whole gallons of iced tea. Not lemonade."

But the room was empty. He saw that the bare floor had some soil on it, from her shoes, and he told himself that it would be a good way to tell when she'd come into the house again—when he saw dirt on the bare wood floor.

"I'm sorry," he said. He wanted to weep, but he was all dried up from exhaustion, so his eyes merely itched. He rubbed them with the back of his hand; it made the itch worse. "I'm sorry," he repeated. And felt a cold numbness in his stomach, as if he were hungry but didn't want to eat.

315

He said again, "I'm sorry," and went downstairs and sat at the kitchen table to get some more waiting done.

"This is Orchid Street, my dear, and you are welcome here."

"Very welcome here."

"We can give you what we can give you . . ."

". . . maybe some comfort . . ."

". . . some peace . . ."

". . . and quiet."

"We're all very good at peace and quiet, you know."

"Though not very good at warmth."

"I think."

"And keep an eye out for the caretaker."

"He skulks about."

"He's always skulking about."

"He thinks he's evil."

"Very evil."

"And maybe he is."

"Who is?"

"Mia mardre!"

"And a drowsy numbness . . ."

"But please forgive the confusion, my dear, forgive the confusion. Some tea perhaps, some lemonade, perhaps, some idle chitchat . . ."

"*. . . pains my sense/As though of hemlock I had drunk . . .*"

"You see, you're our first visitor."

"No, not the first."

"*You look tired, my dear, very . . .*"

Chapter Forty

Five days. It had almost been enough. Five days
with the resurrected and the reshaped. Drinking
lemonade and quoting Keats.

And shriveling up.

Slipping happily into a past that's friendly and
peaceful and seductive. Always seductive.

Watching the skin go pale and the hands move
slowly, very slowly, and the darkness slide in.
And feeling thankful for it, so very thankful for
it.

"Katherine?"

Five days watching the sun come up and pass
across the sky, watching the light come and go,
watching the buildings shimmer and change . . .

Five days with the resurrected and the reshaped, drinking lemonade and quoting Keats.

"Katherine?"

319

And shriveling up, into a past that's friendly and peaceful and seductive.

As if death were the only gift that life could give.

"Katherine?"

Feeling the cold seep in because the always-so-seductive past is not at all good at warmth. Feeling the fingers lighten and the feet stop. Watching the skin go pale and the buildings shimmer and change. And crumble.

Drinking lemonade and quoting Keats with the dead.

"Katherine? Are you awake?"

Grinding nearly to a halt there on the cold, hard earth, moaning that it is not enough, after all, not nearly enough, and slipping back, through the narrow street, pulling something out from deep inside it, something that can animate, something whole. And alive.

"Katherine, are you awake?"

Hearing a curse spill out there, on the street.

"Katherine? I'm sorry."

"Yes."

"I'm so sorry."

"I forgive you."

Watching the street fall away.

"I'm here, Katherine."

Watching the street fold into the earth again.

Watching the dead slip back and the smiles fade, their seduction done.

"I'm here, Katherine."

Their seduction failed.

"I forgive you."

"I waited, Katherine. I brought you back."

"Thank you."

"I'll bring you some tea—"

"But go now."

"Some tea with lemon and honey . . ."

Hearing the voices again, the seduction: "You are welcome here, very welcome here. . . ."

"I love you, Katherine. I have always loved you. I'm sorry."

"This is Orchid Street, and you are welcome here."

"We can give you what we can give you . . ."

". . . maybe some comfort . . ."

". . . some peace . . ."

". . . and quiet."

"We're all very good at peace and quiet, you know."

"Though not at warmth."

"I think."

"I don't have much to give you, Katherine—"

Feeling the anger build and the resolve take hold. Hearing it erupt. "Damn you, goddamn you! I want to be left alone. I want you to leave me alone. I don't need you any more, Larry! I don't *need* you any more!"

Becoming aware, after a while, of the silence in the house. And loving it.

"I don't *need* you anymore!"

Sitting down and drinking lemonade and quoting Keats with the dead.

And pushing the dead away.

And choosing life.

And being whole, at last.

T. M. WRIGHT

LAUGHING MAN

In their own way, the dead tell Jack Erthmun so much. Jack is a New York City police detective with his own very peculiar ways of solving homicides, and those ways are beginning to frighten his colleagues. He gets results, but at what cost? This may be Jack's last case. He's assigned to a series of unspeakable killings, gruesome murders with details that make even seasoned detectives queasy. But as he goes deeper into the facts of the case, facts that make it seem no human killer can be involved, Jack begins to get more and more erratic. Is it the case that's affecting Jack? Or is it something else, something no one even dares to consider?

DONALD BEMAN
AVATAR

When Sean MacDonald first meets sculptor Monique Gerard, he is fascinated. Her work is famous—some would say notorious—for its power, sensuality . . . and unbridled horror. But Sean didn't expect the reclusive genius to be as compellingly grotesque as her creations. Something about her and her work draws Sean in like a moth to a flame . . . or like a lamb to the slaughter.

__4376-9 $5.50 US/$6.50 CAN

MOON
ON THE
WATER
MORT CASTLE

It's a strange world—one filled with the unexpected, the chilling. It's our world, but with an ominous twist. This is the world revealed by Mort Castle in the brilliant stories collected here—our everyday lives seen in a new and shattering light. These stories show us the horror that may be waiting for us around the next corner or lurking in our own homes. Through these disquieting tales you will discover a world you thought you knew . . . and a darker one you'll never forget.

THE
RESTLESS
DEAD
HUGH B. CAVE

A curse lingers over the Everol mansion—a voodoo curse, born of evil, steeped in blood. The tormented family who lives in this house of horrors is beset by insanity, visions . . . and death. They have shut themselves off from the world, allowing no one to trespass on their blighted property. No one except Jeff Gordon, a university professor with a special knowledge of voodoo and the occult. Reluctantly, in desperation, the Everol family has permitted Gordon to enter the mansion. But all Gordon's experience could never prepare him for the unearthly creatures that await him there—or the ultimate terror of the mysterious caves beneath the house.

THE INFINITE

DOUGLAS CLEGG

Harrow is haunted, they say. The mansion is a place of tragedy and nightmares, evil and insanity. First it was a madman's fortress; then it became a school. Now it lies empty. An obsessed woman named Ivy Martin wants to bring the house back to life. And Jack Fleetwood, a ghost hunter, wants to find out what lurks within Harrow. Together they assemble the people who they believe can pierce the mansion's shadows.

A group of strangers, with varying motives and abilities, gather at the house called Harrow in the Hudson Valley to reach another world that exists within the house. . . . A world of wonders . . . A world of desires . . . A world of nightmares.
